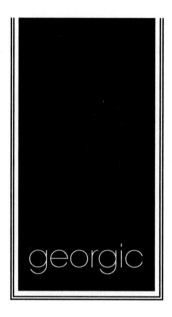

georgic

ALSO BY MARIKO NAGAI

Histories of Bodies

MARIKO 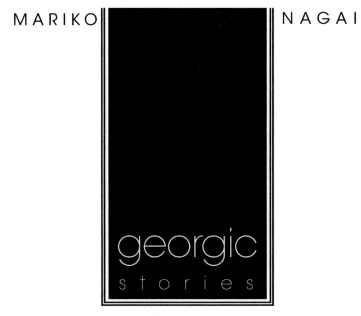 NAGAI

georgic
s t o r i e s

Winner of the
G.S. Sharat Chandra Prize for Short Fiction
selected by Jonis Agee

BkMk Press
University of Missouri-Kansas City

The G. S. Sharat Chandra Prize for Short Fiction wishes to thank preliminary judges Leslie Koffler, Evan McNamara, Linda Rodriguez, and Jane Wood.

BkMk Press also wishes to thank Karla Deel, Sarah Eyer, Heather Inness, Noelle P. Jones, Deirdre Mikolajcik, and Paul Tosh.

Previous winners of the G.S. Sharat Chandra Prize for Short Fiction: *A Bed of Nails* by Ron Tanner, selected by Janet Burroway; *I'll Never Leave You* by H. E. Francis, selected by Diane Glancy; *The Logic of a Rose* by Billy Lombardo, selected by Gladys Swan; *Necessary Lies* by Kerry Neville Bakken, selected by Hilary Masters; *Love Letters from a Fat Man* by Naomi Benaron, selected by Stuart Dybek; *Tea and Other Ayama Na Tales* by Eleanor Bluestein, selected by Marly Swick; *Dangerous Places* by Perry Glasser, selected by Gary Gildner.

Library of Congress Cataloging-in-Publication Data
Nagai, Mariko.
Georgic : stories / Mariko Nagai.
p. cm.
Winner of the G.S. Sharat Chandra Prize for Short Fiction.
Summary: "These stories, based on Japanese folktales and history are all tied to agricultural life, and depict themes of survival through famine, war, religious persecution, and sexual slavery"—Provided by publisher.
ISBN 978-1-886157-76-7 (pbk. : alk. paper)
I. Title.
PR9515.9.N34G46 2010
823'.92—dc21
2010038966

This book is set in Avant Garde Gothic Standard and Garamond Premier Pro.

For my mother

Her children arise up,
and call her blessed;
her husband also,
and he praiseth her.

—Proverbs 31:28

acknowledgments

Grateful acknowledgment is made to the following journals in which some of the stories in this collection first appeared, some in slightly different versions: *The Chattahoochee Review* "Autobiography"; *The Cortland Review* "The Drowning Land"; *New Letters* "Grafting" and "Confession"; *Painted Bride Quarterly Website* "How We Touch the Ground, How We Touch" and "Fugue."

"Grafting" was reprinted in *The Pushcart Prize XXVI* (2002).

Many thank you's to the following residencies and institutions: Hedgebrook Foundation, La Napoule Art Foundation, Ledig House/Art Omi, Temple University Japan Campus and the Corporation of Yaddo for providing me with time and space to conceive, write, and revise stories in this collection, and to Weslyan Writers Conference for a fellowship to attend it. Special gratitude to colleagues at TUJ, especially to Drs. Phil Deans, Kathleen Pike, and Matthew Linley for awarding me TUJ Research and Creative Funds; to the amazing librarians at Temple University Japan for finding obscure articles and books; Daniel de Roulet for the French translation; Jeffrey Kingston for being a fellow writer and lover of good food; Amy Kirsten, "story is a gift," but so is music; Elizabeth Kostova; Sharmistha Mohanty, for friendship cultivated over many cups of afternoon tea in Mandelieu-la Napoule, Delhi, and Hong Kong; Silvia Pareschi for the intercontinental friendship that started at Ledig and continues on, even after five years; Daniel Straub, a fellow traveler; Jonathan Wu for our many nights of dinners and for his patient ears— "this is who we are"; and Dominic Ziegler for his generous heart.

georgic
s t o r i e s

foreword

Mariko Nagai reimagines the georgic, a pastoral form pertaining to rural life, to create a searing portrait of the cost of war, social and political strife, with sadness sharp enough to cut the tongue and grief so unbearable, the journey toward new life so remarkable—it takes your breath to see such tenderness and truth. Through the palpable beauty of the natural world that envelopes the struggles of her characters, Nagai reveals the most profound mysteries of living and dying.

Nagai has a voice and vision to be reckoned with. There is wisdom here, ancient and modern. It has never left us, it simply awaits the discoverer who cannot turn away, who must not let history be rewritten, who must bear witness as each generation has, to the cruelties and kindnesses, the observances that shape our lives.

These stories will change you, change what you know, change how to imagine the lives of people around you. To read Nagai's tales is to remember why we always need stories, especially in times of war, when our humanity is so at risk, especially now.

—Jonis Agee
Final Judge
G. S. Sharat Chandra Prize for Short Fiction

Incline your ear, and come unto me:
Hear, and your soul shall live.

— Isaiah 55:3

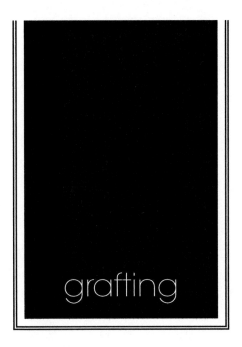

grafting

Harvest. Another failure. Third year in a row. Now. The posted sign in the village center: All people unable to work must leave within two weeks. Children exempted.

The summer had been too long. The short rain season followed by overwhelming heat, sucking every drop of moisture, cracking the earth. The ground opened in the field like mouths waiting for water that never came. We waited for rain. It never came. The green wilted before our eyes. We were helpless. And gods did not hear our prayers this summer; the head had settled too near the earth, sucking our prayers as soon as they came out.

The village was quiet this summer. Everyone hid, afraid to breathe deeply. Cattle died. Their limbs fleshless, taut skin over bones, skeletal, even ghost-like while alive. We were no better than them, our flesh hung loosely around us;

bellies grumbled loudly like a nearing storm. Hands shook; sometimes, we became so lightheaded that we forgot where we were, for an instant, but not long enough to forget that we were hungry. The communal rice bins became lower and lower until we could see the bottom—this summer, no children dared to go to the stream because they knew that they would find only a shallow, muddy puddle at the bottom of a deep crevice. Where the stream once was. A wound of the earth, we call it around here. A deep scar. Third crop failure in a row.

Now the sign. Now, old people must leave.

I tried to tear off the sign before anyone read it. Before anyone woke up. But it was too late. When I got there, women were wailing in each others' arms; men stood with downcast eyes. They had all read the post. And they understood. Their backs said more than words; their backs hung in resignation, in acceptance. We knew. We had known all along. We had known that something like this would happen. Somehow, something or someone must be sacrificed in order for the rest to live. If they stayed, if our old people stayed, we would all be hungry. More than hungry.

We were hungry the first year. We were cold, but somehow we managed. Last year was even worse; we were hungrier than a year before, and we were colder, but somehow, we managed again. But with a heavy price. One by one, the girls left the village. Strange men came from afar with heavy wallets in their hands, as if they knew—bad news travels quicker than the good ones—and the girls went with them, one by one. Hanging their necks, their necks bobbing with sobs. Not one disobeyed their parents; not one tried to escape. They were not yet women. Some of them haven't even had their first bleeding. Most of them would never live to be my age; most of them would never go past twenty-five. Their breasts would be forced into growth under the constant sucking; their breasts would grow under the touches of strangers. And after all these men, what would become of these girls? They all bore it like women, and they didn't even know what it meant. I know which one has a mole between her shoulder blades. I know which one has a scar on her neck. I know all the marks each brought to this world. I saw them come to this world, this cruel and exacting world.

And I miss them. No one talked about them after they left. Some of the parents erased the names from their doors, erasing them from their daily lives. They were banished even from our memory. But money from selling a daughter can go only so far. It never lasts. When spring came, we sighed in relief. We finally breathed. We ate roots and grasses, pretending them to be feasts fit for the nobleman. It's easy to lie, really; the mind and body are easily fooled. We prayed earnestly. We all did. But gods were busy, or indifferent, I do not know. And we were hungry. More than we wanted to admit.

So now, this again.

The only way to eliminate hunger is by cutting down the number of mouths. Old people. They cannot stand up straight. They cannot raise anything heavy over their shoulders; they cannot even raise their own arms. Some cannot see farther than their fingers; some cannot hear our loudest whispers. There are some, like my mother, who don't remember their lives.

My mother doesn't remember my name. My mother doesn't remember much of her life. She lives in a different time than I do—sometime before I was born, perhaps even before she herself was born. But somehow, wherever she is, whenever she is, she seems content. Contained in her world.

Or, perhaps, worlds. Perhaps she lives in many worlds, all of it better than where we are, where I am.

She bridged the other world and this one, a midwife. Every man in this village had come through the mother's canal and fell into my mother's hands. Sometimes, she coaxed the baby because they did not want to leave the other world. They were stubborn in their refusal, but she lured them out, somehow, with promises of sweet things this world offers. Cold water against the bare skin, the feeling of wet grass under bare feet, how laughter could never be explained with words. She helped with everyone's birth here until her hands hardened like hands on the woodcarvings, and she could no longer feel women's insides. She said that fingers must be delicate, must be flexible because women's insides are delicate and fragile. Then her memories began to leave her one by one, as if the doors of cages of canaries opened, birds taking flight timidly, then boldly one by one. First, what medicine she is mixing in the bowl. Then, the names of the pregnant mothers. Then her own name. The birds each took something of her past. Now, she is left with nothing. The birds keep flying away, one by one, each minute. The only time she speaks now is when she, somewhere deep inside of her, somewhere most primordial, speaks out of necessity like a baby wailing when in hunger, or wet, and even those cries come out weakly, as if she is not even sure of what she needs herself.

Time leaves her, as quickly as it passes through her. She's living the past as she sits in front of me, asking me questions. The future hasn't happened to her yet, though I know what happens. She lives in a time when the past and present become one. Sometimes, she waves her spotty wooden hands gracefully in the arch, as if she's tracing a train of thought that no one can see. She doesn't say anything; she seems content. She looks like she doesn't need anything else in the world when she's like that. Coaxing her to go for a walk is hard, is simple—I never know when she wants to be led, or to lead, or to stay. When tugging becomes too much, when I pull her too hard, she stubbornly stands where she is, time leaving her quickly, and she can stand there for an hour, for two hours, forever if I let her. Times like that, she looks young for a second, like she's the girl she must have been more than a half a century ago, her eyes sparkling like a pair of shiny stones on the bottom of the stream. She seems to enjoy her own stubbornness. It's beautiful to see her when she's like that. She is a child, mine, as I was hers, and I love her because she doesn't remember anything. Because she cannot see how she is now.

She, too, must leave.

The villagers come to me one by one, late at night. They ask what they should do, what we should do. *We have no more daughters to sell; we have nothing to eat. And this is only the beginning, we survived eating roots in spring... must we all die? Must we all die?* I cannot tell them anything. They have sold their daughters; their daughters will live for ten years at most, domesticated beasts, really. Their insides will rot with each year they are penned in the bedrooms and back rooms of inns and bars that sell women more than alcohol. But these villagers have sold their daughters so that they can live just for a season. I sent them away with a quiet blessing, a packet of herbal tea or a carved branch, anything just to quiet them. Tell them that these charms will give them the answer. They do not want an answer; they just want someone to agree with them. Anything I tell them, they will turn deaf ears. They will not have enough courage to kill their parents; they will take their parents up to the mountain and leave them. So they will die somewhere away from them, somewhere they cannot see. As they did their daughters.

My mother will have to leave. I will have to carry her on my back, go up to the mountain to the waterfall and leave her with the others. So they will not starve, so they will not go thirsty, so they will not die alone; they will live, so the villagers say, they will live longer than we will, the villagers say. And they say many things more. Many many more. And there are only twelve nights left before I, too, leave her.

She sleeps. In one of her many worlds. Her mouth open slightly, she looks like a child in her deep prayer. A look of deep concentration. She moves slightly. I turn away from her sleeping body. The villagers may not have mercy, but I, too, have no mercy. I would rather take my mother somewhere I cannot see her, have her fight for a short life rather than to strangle her in her sleep. Or smother her.

It's easy. It must be easy. A pillow over her face, it will not take too long. It must be easy to kill a child without a common memory. I have seen so many mothers do it to their children, infants, umbilical cords still warm and thick. A child without an arm, some that looked too much like cats, their lips split right beneath the nose. *We have angered the fox god, so the child looks like a fox. What kind of future would she have?* One child, I remember, did not have legs or arms, its head grotesquely open like a crushed pomegranate. The mother cried, she had cried and cried as she put a pillow over its misshapen head. It did not struggle. It just accepted, tiny chest rising and rising, and slowly, slower and slower until it stopped moving. It left without a memory, perhaps only the memory of its mother's cry that did not end. The mother died a few days later. We found her body in the village well, her belly bloated as if she were once again pregnant. The villagers had kicked her body around, kicked until her belly burst. They left her carcass for the crows to pick on. *That bitch fouled our water supply*, they cursed; *now we have to walk so far to get*

the water from the stream. I took her body back to her family
before anything got to her. They did not take the body; they
just told me to let it rot. I buried her in my yard. My mother
had looked at the ground and smiled. She even placed a wild
chrysanthemum on the grave. All the babes came and went,
lived for a minute, two minutes, then disappeared. From one
world to another.

Will it be that easy? It will be easer than knowing that
she will live without me, looking for me. It will be short. Her
cry under the pillow will be muffled. It will be short. It will
have to be short, two minutes at most. She is so weak she will
not be able to fight me.

I take my pillow from my bed and stand over her.

She opens her eyes. It is clear; it is like the way I remember her eyes before her past flew away. She whispers, "I heard
what they said. Take me to the mountain," then she closes
her eyes.

The next day, day after, I look at my mother. That night
must have been a dream, a waking dream, I tell myself. One
by one, the old people disappear from the village. The children have grown sullen and quiet. They know. Their eyes are
unusually calm with redness.

A scream from one house, a scream so mournful, so much
like a pig about to get slaughtered. An old man runs as fast as
he can from the yard. He is half-blind, but rocks and the un-
even road mean nothing to him now. He runs past me. His
son catches up with him. The old man yells, *Help me, please. I
don't want to leave my home. How can you do this to me? How
can you banish me, just like that? I won't eat, I promise I won't
eat; just let me die here. Just let me die where I was born.* His
son cries. His grandchildren stand by the gate, looking at the
play with startlingly calm eyes. Then the son hits the bald
wrinkled head with an axe, the blunt side lightly on the side

of the old head. Not hard enough to kill, but hard enough to quiet. The old man crumbles. The son cries. He cries like the child he once was. The son has no mercy. He cannot even kill his father with his own hands. He'd rather let the father die alone, so far away from the home.

I avert my eyes. I make my way home. My mother lies in her bed, staring at the ceiling as if there is a universe right there, right in front of her face. Her mouth gaped open, lips caved in without the teeth. Cheeks sunken in. She is somewhere else today.

I get the bathwater ready. Keeping one eye on my mother, I stir the bathwater, evening the hot and cold, my reflection on the water swirling, swirling until it is only a blended colored blur.

Stand up, Mama, stand up, I say, nudging my mother with my hand. She looks blankly at the ceiling. I lift the blanket from her; I get her on her legs slowly. She wobbles like a young animal learning to walk for the first time, a newborn doe taking its first step.

That's right, Mama, that's right, slowly, slowly, we're going to take a nice bath today, you like a bath, don't you, yes, we're taking a bath, I say. I talk to her as if she is a baby, though she is far from being a child, a beautiful child, my baby. My mother stands with her legs apart, bent knees, her back slumped. The robe has become undone, already half-naked as she stands. One of her breasts exposed, her breast that hangs low around her wrinkled stomach. Her flesh hangs loosely around her, colorless, flesh hanging loosely. The cloth around her hip is already soiled from a half day of lying down, heavy in my hand. Leading her slowly to the bathroom, one step at a time—she is obedient today, an obedient child.

Yes, Mama, one step at a time, one step, I coo, and she seems happy to oblige. I lift her up; I lift her into the bathroom, the body shaven into less than half, less than one-third of what it used to be, shaven down to the bare essential, a grafted tree. Even privacy—what sets us apart from beasts —is taken from her; her shame is for all to see, her shame no longer her shame, but mine. My mother lies on her back, lies on her back as she did on her bed, floating in water, her body weighing nothing on my hand in water. She does not resist the water like the young body; nor does it let go like the dead body. Her eyes keep looking at the ceiling; she does not see me, she does not see anything except what she can only see, somewhere inside of her.

I pack the essentials. This robe, that thick jacket for cold nights, each cloth bringing me closer to the common memory my mother and I share. Forget long enough, but not long enough. Outside on the street, I see a villager with an old woman on his back, a ragged sack, really. The old woman sits on the broad back. She looks around and, as if she is shying away from remembering, of too much remembrance, she glances around lightly, just enough to remember the outlines of the village, but not the details. Our eyes meet. She nods at me. She is wearing her best robe. They walk toward north, where the mountain waits. Where other old people wait, where others will join, even my mother.

I take my mother's hand; I tell her that it is time to go. She grasps it, hard. My knuckles turn white.

I strap her on my back, binding us hard with a belt. Binding us together.

The path becomes thinner and thinner. Thin line, wide enough for the sole. The past travelers seem indecisive; the path is crooked, veering left for no reason, then tightly curving right. I carry her on my back, and soon, she falls asleep, trusting all her weight on me. Her face nestles on my back, her breath rising and falling on my hair that has become undone. How far must I carry her before I must abandon her?

The night closes in, and the path starts to fade into darkness. She wakes up and says that she is hungry. Stopping where we are, I spread her bed next to mine; we make a small fire and cook a little rice in the pan. She opens her mouth while I am cooking, waiting for me to feed her. She opens her mouth, not closing it while I feed her little by little.

Then I tell her that we must rest. *Sleep*, I tell her, *sleep*. And she does.

The next day is like the day before. I carry her on my back. She is making a soft sound, a mewling sound, gently opening her hands, then closing them.

I let her be. She is happy where she is. The mountain is close enough, in front of us.

We enter the thickets of trees the next day. She is becoming heavier and heavier. All the past she carries with her weighs me down. My feet do not go as fast as they did when we set out. The belt binding us together must be rebound every hour, becomes loose from my mother falling off of my back slowly, slowly, an inch every minute. The mountain is in front of us.

Each tree we pass, she bends the branch, breaks it enough that the branch still hangs with the rest. I ask her what she is doing.

"For you to get back without getting lost."

She continues to do so, even after I tell her that I know my way back, I know *our* way back. She reaches over to the branch her height, no more than the height of my own shoulder, splinters each branch as a landmark. I will be the only one to see it.

I cannot see the villagers before me or behind me; they have not come this way. I don't know where they have taken the old people. Maybe we have lost our way already. I have never gone through this path. She does not care. She continues to bend the branch, lets it hang there.

The path slopes upward. It is no longer a path but a trail of beasts. But beasts never walk in uniformity the way we do. They roam where they want; they are not creatures of habit. Habits will kill them. They follow a certain rhythm, but no more. Habits will mark them into weakness; they will be caught by predators or hunger if they followed the same path each day of their lives.

The back of my mother is bruised. There are blue X marks on my chest from the rope. The blisters on my feet have burst. I have discarded my sandals.

My mother has refused to be on my back today. As I tried to put her on my back, she stood there, twenty minutes, thirty minutes.

Mama, please, get on my back, Mama. Mama, please, please, I coo.

No one answers me.

She tugs my shoulder.

My mother comes no higher than my shoulders, but she is stronger. She leads me by my hand, her hand tugging strongly. Her feet so light I think about squirrels.

We rest.

She is restless. She continues to break the branches. Our supply is getting low.

We start. I have lost count of how many days we have been traveling like this, this aimless travel, this journey that must end eventually, like her life.

We must be somewhere near the clearing. We see more light. The leaves, green-yellow, green-red, seem brighter. I know that we are near the end. I now lead, all the tiredness gone. All the worries gone.

We reach the clearing. It is beautiful. Somewhere close by, there must be a stream running by. There's a little concave hollow there, a huge boulder jutting out to provide a shelter. I know this is where my mother will live.

I tell her that this is where we will rest for a while, and I begin to gather twigs to build a fire. Taking out the pot, and boiling the last supply of rice I brought with us, she helps me as much as she can, though her gnarled hands cannot hold anything properly. Her hands just wave around as if she is cooking herself, but she is nowhere near me. That is enough —that she wants to help. She seems a bit distant. She has left me again.

I feed her in silence.

As I lay out her clothing near her, she leans against the rock, looking far ahead.

Mama, let's play hide-and-seek, OK? You be the it, and I'll hide, is that OK? Mama, are you listening? You be the it, start counting one... two... three... OK? I tell her.

She looks at me blankly, then something in her flickers in recognition.

Yes, Mama, like this, one... two... three... you say it, Mama, I say.

One... two... my mother opens her mouth as much as she can as if she is actually saying the number.

I want to touch her before I hide. I reach over, then stop. *Six... Seven...* I begin to run across the clearing, toward the thicket we had exited from. *Ten... Eleven...* I count in my head. I cannot see where I am going, except that I must follow the broken twigs on the tree. *Seventeen... Eighteen...* I run as fast as I can.

Twenty... I run down the path. The path to the village will take more than fifty counts. The village. It must be nearly deserted. I can go back, not reminded of my mother because there will be no old people to remind me of her. She will be erased, as the other old people have been erased, disappeared from history as the houses disappear in darkness. But what of the morning? When the light brings about the disappeared houses? Will we be reminded? Can we ever erase our past? The daughters may be gone, somewhere far in the big cities, selling their nights to strange men, but I remember. The mother could not forget the limbless child; she killed herself. And everyone else wanted to forget her, even her family; everyone wanted to forget the shame she had brought when she killed herself, when she gave birth to the monster. But they still remember her. She will not go away.

I stop. I strain my ears to hear the count.

Thirty-nine... forty.

I close my eyes. I am no different from the villagers. I can say that I am different, that I am not like them. The villagers who can sell their daughters to survive for a season, a mere season; the villagers who can abandon their old parents. How different am I? My story is like theirs. Our stories are the same. I am no different. I am here, where they are. Or, have been. In the mountain. With my mother. I am no different.

Forty-three... forty-four... I begin to walk. Where I came from. Where my mother is. *Forty-seven... forty-eight...* I begin to walk faster. *Forty-nine... fifty...* the leaves turn brighter and brighter. I stand by the tree closest to the clearing.

My mother stands in the middle of the clearing. Her arms in front of her as if she is searching for something in the dark. This darkness, this darkness that has invaded our lives for a long time. Not caring that her robes have become loose in motion.

I stand, quiet.

A bird whistles by. The wind rustles the trees. And my mother stands still with her back bent, her arms in front of her. Her robes flap around her, wings of a bird about to take a flight if it could.

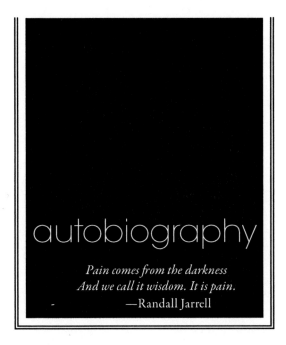

autobiography

Pain comes from the darkness
And we call it wisdom. It is pain.
—Randall Jarrell

If this were another time and another land, if gods were kinder or heard your prayer, your child would be twelve now—her face taking on the reminiscence of your own. Each part of her would have been a reminder that you had given birth to her, even the slightest way in which she cocked her neck, as if she were listening to voices other than what was apparent, real. But no longer.

You have sold her. You have not told anyone.
No one knows. No one must know.

Someone will tell us your story if you do not: in another land, in another land, a war ended. Your husband had been drafted at the last minute, and you were left, without money or language to survive. The only luggage, the only things you had time to gather up were the clothes on your body and a child, an infant really, who would not stop crying. Not during the evacuation south to where the border lay, and neither in the shelter where you nested for a season, temporary and barren like the feeding place of a migrating bird. They kept telling you to bash the child's head against the ground, to strangle its small neck while it slept, just to shut the child up, *just shut the brat up, they'll find us out, shut her up*, and you were helpless, unable to find food to feed yourself so that you could feed the child in your arms. You sold your body so that you could continue to provide milk. Night or day, you lay on your back with your legs open, men entering you for the price of a slice of bread—the price had been deflated, you see, and women were no longer expensive, no longer a commodity that could be translated into value of any sort. There were more than "enough women around for the few men left. And men wanted money, food, not women." These meals you earned were not enough to fill up the hunger, but enough to keep going, to keep living, to keep breathing until the border opened up and you could ride the boat across the short distance of ocean.

Then one day, your child stopped crying and began to whimper. You could not do anything. Your breasts no longer held milk; your body began to eat itself from inside. When you looked down at your own body, in those moments between men, you saw a hard and brittle fishbone on your chest, but these were your own ribs. The chants, *sell us your children, sell us your children*, kept going; you were desperate. The child was dying; there was nothing you could do. So you sold the child. You sold her to a faceless, nameless voice of the night so that she could be better fed, better looked after, so that she could have a chance to live. You bought yourself a passage on the boat to go back home with that money. You shed your past, remarried, and lived the rest of your life trying not to remember.

If a biographer were to write your life in one sentence, it would be this: a woman sold her child so that she could return home. They'd write it like that, without details, without the intricate movement of happiness and despair and darkness that fills up between the silent lines of a story.

But you are telling this story; it is your turn.

Here is what happened: the border bends, unable to hold back the force pushing in from outside. The enemy pushes and pushes until it breaks, changing the map of the world. Your husband is drafted at the very last minute, and he dies in the northern lands, where winter never ends, and he dies thinking of hunger, of cold. His death is not heroic or mythical in proportion; he dies a very human death. You would like to believe that he died honorably, but you also know that soldiers seldom do.

He is dead, him and the rest of the soldiers who are better fit for farming, for growing. You are left with your only child, an infant you must look after. You are the only one alive, except for the child who trusts all her weight in her sleep, indifferent to the forces of history, indifferent to your fear.

You do everything to survive. You sell your body. You beg. These things can be written in few words, but they contain more than that. They are beyond words, and once you experience it, you know that words cannot carry all the weight of shame and guilt and desperation that you go through.

And now, your child is dying in your arms. You have no one to cling to or to blame for the hunger. Everyone is hungry. When you eat, if you do, the food is so old, the portions so small, that nothing stays. And in return, your child rejects everything that enters her. You begin to think that your breasts are poisoned. Everything comes out immediately as it enters her, and the wastes that comes out of her immediately freeze, gluing her to the ground. Every morning, you have to peel her body off the ground. Her body is small and weak. She is like a fly struggling to free itself from sticky paper.

Your hands are chapped, tattered from the cold, and your child cries every time you touch her. The child becomes helpless and less resistant to death, lies there as if she is learning to accept her own fate. And the voices grow insistent, *Sell us your children! Sell us your children! You are starving them to death for some selfish reason. Give them a chance to live. A better mother would wish for life, not death.* The voices croon, as if they were singing a Big Band song, and you almost want to believe them.

Children are sold. It is not necessity that propels mothers around you. It is love.

She is mine. She is no one else's. I must choose her life for her because she cannot. Late one night, your hands fly around the child's neck. Two thumbs cross at her small Adam's apple—the throat god, they call it where you come from. Then you concentrate all of your strength, all the love you can muster, on the tips of your thumbs. A quick death. That is the only way to do this. The child's eyes bulge, then her arms raise themselves over her face as if she is blinding herself.

And you stop.

Instead, you hurriedly wrap her up in a small bundle, bury your face against her neck that smells of urine and waste and death and age, a smell too old for her. Carrying her, you run outside, where the voices wait, where the future waits expectantly. You give her to one of the voices—it did not matter which one—as you keep repeating her name over and over into her ears. Thrusting her small body into a pair of waiting arms, you entrust her future to a stranger. By repeating her name, your return her name and her life to her.

Now, you can live your life. Left with nothing. No past, but only a pocketful of money—enough for a one-way ticket out of this land. When you somehow make your way back to your mother, she asks you what has happened to your baby, and you tell her that she died. Very simply. You will not tell her, *I have killed her in my mind so that I could live on, so that she could live on. Even if it means she'd live the rest of her life hating me for abandoning her, it is better to be able to hate than to be dead, without hate.*

You keep your silence and you remarry.

You tell yourself that letting go of a child is nothing hard. It is nothing new. History is littered with abandoned offspring and orphans, displaced children without mothers or country to claim as their own. It is easy to let go.

But it is not. It is easy to pretend to forget, but you can never forget. In the dark nights, you hear her cry when the winter wind sneaks between spaces. At times like that, when cries become too loud, when your child appears in darkness, you bury yourself into your new husband's body, tell him to fill you so. *So that I can bear another child to fill up the space she left, so I can forget about another body I lay with in a different land. There is a child who came before you, who came before all these children we have had between us. Let me forget that land.* And you welcome the man, you welcome the new life with your legs open like arms wide open to embrace a new love.

This is what happened.

Others, who do not know, nor ever understand your past, they will say that you are a model wife, a model mother. They

will see amidst the etched face, dried from being out in the
sun, long hours of tilling the earth, and they will say, look
how the land has ravished her face, but she is beautiful still. If
they are to see your palms, they will claim your life fortunate,
unmarred by misfortunes and fickle gods. They will not see
how the rivers are dry, how the streams are cut in the middle
twice: one for the husband no one talks about and one for
the child who may still live in another country, blaming you
for her fate.

You left your life with her in another land, and what is
left of your life is the life of least resistance, life of obedience
and regularity.

Your new husband knows nothing. He is happy with
you, and you let him be. Your children are provided for, but
their lives are important to you in a formal way. Once you
had decided on your life, living it became irrelevant and perhaps distant like that foreign land.

You want to imagine that her new parents never told her
that she was not their own; you want to imagine, too, that
they told her of her real name, and that she was yours. She
may not understand your love for her, what made you thrust
her into the arms of new parents for a bundle of money. She
may also never understand that love comes in many faces.
That love may transform itself into the unrecognizable, monstrous, and mysterious. She may never understand all that.
Or she may.

You imagine the way she looks now, after twelve years,
and you hope that she lives happily, as much as anyone can
be happy. You imagine all her pain, all the sadness, of the
first love, of the first heartbreak; you imagine. When the sun
beats on your back as you bend down to the ground, seeding

the ground for next season, you tell yourself that there was no choice: you could not bear to watch her die. You could not bear to be helpless. You were weak; that your love for your child was stronger than, than what? But now, this is your secret. No one must know, not your new husband, not your new children. You revised your life the moment you sold your child: your first marriage never happened. There was no child before this marriage. A revised life.

You do not know that your husband lies next to you at night, thinking of lying with someone else, someone less severe, someone more accessible, someone that he loves. And your children, these children that will grow up tilling the earth, these children will later look back and wonder if they have ever been held. They will say amongst themselves, *she was a good mother*, but they will never utter, *she loved us*. They will say, *there was always a distance between us, as if she were somewhere else, as if she left a part of herself somewhere.*

And you imagine this: if she comes to you now, searching for you, her name remembered, you will not tell her of your hardened chest, of the love that has always been there. You will not tell her how you have lain in the arms of the new man, betraying her over and over each time you bore a child, how you dared not name each new child after her. You will look at her straight in her eyes. You will not tell her of the passage back, how you kept calling out her name on the ship, trying to throw her away each time, but how her name would not come out. You will not tell her that you are sorry. You will not tell her any of this.

Instead, you will look at her straight, and you will ask her who she is.

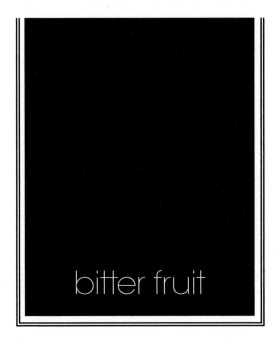

bitter fruit

Monkey did not cry the first time a man entered her. Donned in a red nightgown, Monkey understood what she was, if not what she had to do; the Madam, her *Mother,* had told her what she was expected to do when she first arrived here in this house. Coyly lowering her piercing eyes, the Madam said, *When a man thing enters, you will surely feel pain, but it is nothing to be scared of. Every woman must go through pain to become a woman. Next thing you know, you will be begging for more and more until you can't live without it. For an ugly whore like you, you'd be lucky if a man loved you enough to pay you.*

Remembered words the Madam, her *Mother,* had said to her when she first arrived flew around like panicking birds as she sat by the window, where men gazed in. As she caught glimpses of them walking by, their bodies strangely cut horizontally by the trellis, she lightly grasped two bars with the tips of her fingers. There seemed to be no end to the streaming of men; for a moment, the current ended, and what remained was the window opposite hers, where women sat motionless like dolls, waiting, their thickly powdered faces betraying no emotion except for identical red lips that occasionally curled and wriggled like freshly dug worms. *Worm*, Monkey thinks. A worm has dug itself through her body, and she pushed aside the thought.

It was better than what she had left behind in the village where she came from, she told herself. When the crop failed again—it seemed to her that ever since she could remember, the crop failed each autumn—she knew that *that* year, there was no place left for her in her house, or in the village. She was the only girl left in the family; all her three older sisters had left the village late at night, shrinking into darkness, with feeble promises, of money and glory of return with rich husbands, all of which no one believed. Even the sisters.

They are going to have better lives, her mother said each time they left, her eyes following them out of the door, but never getting up from where she sat. Monkey—that was the prostitute's given name—knew that sweet words snaking out of strange men's mouths, those practiced and oiled words that her parents and others in the village drank greedily like crude wheat gruel, were not to be trusted. It was better, she felt, to be without hunger. Her parents were hungry: for food, for blind faith, for anything that their isolated imaginations could conjure up.

So one late afternoon, when her mother told her to go and see a man waiting for her by the pine tree at the outskirts of the village, she knew that her parents had sold her. Her mother washed her hair, gently stroking it down until no stray strand rebelled. *It's better where you'll be going*, her mother kept combing in the words. And putting aside the comb, her mother took out a boxed rouge. *Here, take this, you will need it where you go.* The rouges they made, but never used. Rouge flowers that tattered the hands, reddened them until fingertips became crudely rouged like the lips of prostitutes. Rouges that prostitutes in the capital smeared on their lips before their own bodies flushed like one big lip, provocatively beckoning the men. Rouge that, from that day on, became the only thing that called up home.

And when she followed the dim path toward the pine tree, when she traced the indecisive path that followed the outline of rice and rouge fields, no one looked at her. Already a ghost who had passed on to the otherworld, she had become invisible, a past, no one had to tell her that she had been erased from the history of the village. She passed by a neighbor. The woman's milky white eyes looked at her briefly, nodded, then looked away quickly as if to ward off evil. And her father, cloth around him loose like a scarecrow's, stood outlined against the mountain in the background. She could see each tree on the mountain, but not her father's expression. He might have nodded. He might have waved. Only that he raised an arm up, then looked down to where he stood to continue plowing the impoverished land.

When she arrived here, a brothel in this walled-in city, after what seemed like weeks and years of walking, after her feet hardened with blisters, her soles thick with mud and hard skin, the Madam took one look at her and burst out laughing.

You should feel grateful that I'm going to let you stay here. If I were a meaner Madam, I'd make you stay in the kitchen until your back is bent and your face covered in wrinkles and spots.

Turning to the man who had brought her here, the Madam coyly raised her eyebrows as she must have done many times, ever since she was younger and had her youth to make men believe that she was attractive—*Let's hope she's a virgin, she has the look of a cheap slut. You didn't... well, touch her, did you?*

The man laughed. *I'd sooner sleep with a monkey before I touch this thing.*

That became her name: Monkey.

And Monkey had not known that she was not pretty. She had been told all her life that she was a good obedient girl. Where she came from, prettiness did not matter; farming required obedience, not beauty.

Then, the wait began. She was washed, she was examined, but no one told her what they were waiting for. Monkey waited for what seemed like one long night, undivided by mornings. In reality, it was three days; the fourth night was the night of the auction. Where she was kept, one dark box, monotony broken by two meager meals and the bathroom break that followed immediately afterward; only then could she see not all, but bits and parts of the house. It seemed all like a dream, an unavoidable dream in which there was no way out, not even light ahead. But not silence. It was never silent. She understood as much as she could, that what they would auction was her body. Other than that, she had no idea. It was an act done in darkness, sometimes what she had heard her parents doing in the small room that six other people shared, the blanket rustling and heavy short breaths that tried to be quieter.

And what awaited her at the end of the wait were faces of a few old men, looks of hunger erasing any traces of humanness. Having eaten with a never-ending supply of drinks, the old men sat around, relaxed, accompanied by this or that prostitute tangled around their necks, already half-dressed, makeup already smeared, their red underclothes exposed. With a formal bow and a cry of "Let us begin," the mistress looked around for bets to start flying around the room. No one yelled. Men looked at each other dubiously, as if they had just realized that a game had started, though they did not know its rules.

One man yelled out, "I heard she was ugly, but no one told me she was this ugly!"

With that, men laughed.

The mistress laughed, too. "What are you talking about Master? She's a fine one. Look at her teeth—nothing missing. Look at her hands—big like a maple leaf. Look especially at her chin—this is the very chin that the masters of old age sang about. Your eyes must be going blind if you can't see her fine, womanly figure."

"I'm not talking about parts of her. With a big mouth like that, she's going to bite off my cock. She's so ugly I can't even get it up."

The mistress looked at the face of the man, then the other men, one by one. Coughing once, then again, she smiled.

"This is a fruit that's the first of the season. An apple at the end of the summer. A tangerine at the end of autumn when the leaves have, all but one, left the trees. You, whoever is lucky and daring enough, would be the first to bite, the first to taste it."

"And be it bitter or sweet, only the first bite tells. You've said the same thing before. I'm not fool enough to take that bite. Why, this fruit looks so bitter that you'd get mouth ache just by looking."

Raising her eyebrow coyly, she looked gently at the man. "Ah, my master, that's where you're mistaken. This fruit, though bitter it may look, is still a fruit nevertheless. The first bite lasts forever for the fruit. And you will be the first one to taste its exquisite taste."

"I'll take one," a man with a collapsed face raised one of his fingers slightly.

"Oh Master, surely a man like you knows that this fruit costs more than that. Imagine, you will be the first one to bite into this fruit."

Another man raised two fingers silently.

"Surely, masters are intelligent. This fruit is worth more than that. Remember when Watermelon first came here? So young and awkward, and with your help, she became the woman who does not shame her name. She is ripe, tasty, her juice overflowing every time there is a touch. She is the artwork you have painstakingly created. You can do that with this girl here."

"But this one isn't a fruit. She's a Monkey. Mistress, you must keep a stable here. You have a Horse, and now a Monkey."

"Ah, master, but Horse was worth breaking, wasn't she?"

"Oh right, after she tried to bite me off, I don't go near her."

"Let's see how ripe this fruit is."

"Ah, master. That's against the rules."

"They do that at other houses—let us see how ripe this is by cutting."

"Be patient, master. With the right price, you can be the first to bite."

But no one raised their fingers. Monkey sat transfixed where she was, following the design of the mat silently. And somehow, the agreement must have been reached after the Mistress' theatrically woeful voice protesting, "But I'll be the laughing stock of the neighborhood with a price like that," and "Don't you pity a woman who must run a business all by herself?" and "Surely, you have been good customers, please, just once, just this once..."

And after that, she was taken to a dimly lit room—the first and last time she was left alone with a man, a private act contained where it belonged. And after a long while, as she sat by the bedding, the door slid behind her slowly.

"Have a wonderful time, sir," the mistress must have smiled.

Unsheathing of cloth. Then a deep, old voice that sounded startlingly like her father's.

"Turn around. Let me look at you."

Monkey's heart fluttered, she almost did what the man told her to, but didn't.

"Are you deaf as well as ugly? I said, turn around and let me see your ugly face."

She slowly turned around, following the vertical line running next to her, with her eyes, slowly until a pair of gnarled brown feet, nails caked with grime, came into view, then a pair of naked white calves covered with dark wiry hair. As she slowly raised her eyes, she did not see legs ending and clothing starting, but only skinny thighs the color of the dead fish's eyes, and atop it, where the thighs met, a small penis the size of a baby mouse that helplessly perched on top of the wrinkled sack, hair sparsely grown.

Monkey averted her eyes quickly.

"Keep looking. Put it in your mouth," and with that, the man grabbed her hair and pushed her face against it, the putrid rotten smell of a dead cow gagging her. She struggled, pushing her arms in front of her to ward it off.

The more she struggled, the harder the grasp around her head, and the bigger the baby mouse grew. Craning its head from the dark underbrush, the mouse grew bigger and bigger, until it was the size of an adult mouse. It wriggled around her closed lips; it tried to force its way into her mouth.

Then with a sudden force, the man pushed her onto her back, then pinned her to the floor. Something hard pressed against her thighs; something jerked her tightly pressed knees apart. Then the intrusion.

"You like that, huh? You like that, say so," the man

grunted on top of her as he frantically kept moving, moving, strands of hair flying all over her face, almost in desperate comical jerks. And he sighed deeply, then stopped moving.

She did not know when he left, or when the mistress arrived. Only when the mistress pulled her hair and jerked her up with a scream, "You've dirtied the bed. It'll be added to your debt. Now get up and start cleaning."

Monkey crawled up. Something trickled down her thighs. It was a white trail smeared with red. Where she was, there was a red stain the size of a rouge flower.

She later found out that what the man paid was less than for a whole trout, the cheapest of fish in the market.

She was worth less than a trout. That was her worth.

Because this neighborhood is confined by three walls and a river, rumors circulated from prostitutes' mouths passed on through self-effacing servants who caught every drop of rumors like hungry fish in a small pond, then back to other prostitutes, stories folded into manifold, catching this or that new detail until the original story seemed disfigured and unrecognizable: Monkey's price—worth less than a trout— became a lesson, a legend, set as the lowest standard for any prostitute, new or old. When a teahouse was assaulted with men with lean wallets, that price was used as a rule to keep these men out—*Well, maybe in some houses, they don't mind a girl's first rite being that cheap, but in our house, we do have standards. All girls come from good families. We're not that desperate, you know. Why don't you go to some of these houses, where your wallet matches the price of girls?* And sometimes, as Monkey entered the bathhouse, even after all these years, she heard water splashing frantically, then whispers so slight it could've been echoes from long time ago, the word left by some phantom woman that no longer existed—*trout, less than a trout.* Nobody at her house ever mentioned it because it was their collective shame, their house forever tainted by the price, the past unforgiving and unmerciful.

In the unspoken hierarchy, she was at the bottom because she was the woman whom men chose not out of choice but out of necessity, when their urges became bigger than what they could afford. When Watermelon and Gingko Leaf, and even Horse—other prostitutes housed in the same house— were chosen through the horizontally barred windows, when no one was left by the window, she sat, still unchosen. There was no average time girls sat by the window, but for Monkey, she was, or felt, that time she sat by the window, that pocket of time between one man and another, seemed longer, more measured than the rest. Watermelon usually had her nights filled a week in advance; she did not take more than two if she could help it. An early night, then another later, after midnight, when what a man wanted was a solid block of time. Gingko Leaf, because she was still young to make up for the roundness of her curves—which would, in her middle age, make her look if not voluptuous, than at least handsome —seemed not to rest between men. As soon as she tried to sit behind the bars, to make herself comfortable, a voice outside would call in, "Are you new? I haven't seen you before." And without actually sitting down, her knees supporting the weight in midair, she would giggle, flutter the edges of her already loosened clothes, her gesture an awkward imitation of Watermelon's, get up, her hand beckoning the man in an unperfected seductive wave. And the man would disappear from vision, only to reappear behind her, behind where they sat, as if drawn by an invisible thread that bound Gingko Leaf and the man for a hurried hour of embrace. All in the eerily red light, all seemed theatrical, too formulaic, as if the movements were already formed and practiced, as if it did not really matter who the actors were as long as they went by the movements already laid out before they were born, even before the gods themselves were created in the minds of some dreamer.

After many seasons, the village, her mother bending down to pick orange-red blossoms, her sisters who wished for better lives, better something, by wishing for husbands —all seemed like a dream, and the only reality she knew was in what she saw every day from behind the trellised wall, where light filtered in horizontally, where everything she saw was obstructed by bars. Her days spent mostly under men, or sometimes on her knees and hands. Her present was intimately connected to the bodies and mechanical desire of men. Only dread followed a night passed without men. It meant that time passed monotonously, as still as a still life painted by painters who visited the walled neighborhood she lived in. But she was not a painter: if she could paint what she saw as she sat behind the barred window, if she had a choice to paint, she wouldn't have anyway. What waited for her at the end of the night, the end of the long night that was never truly dark, when the sun rose, was not a sense of relief, but the piercing words of the Madam and the punishment. *You can't eat unless you've earned the right to eat*, the Madam would say as she stuffed her mouth with food so meager that even monks ate better than her. At times like that, the Madam's face collapsed, everything centering so around the mouth, her lips concave from where her teeth once were.

Not knowing anything except for her parents' desperate act of love, she had become a prostitute. Her mother was wrong: where she was, she did not need the rouge. There was no need: with or without, men entered her. All day long, she sat by the window, following the lines of horizontal bars. From top to bottom, she had learned to measure her day sitting still, memorizing the faintest of wood patterns on each bar. The third one from the top, at the fourth glance from the left, a curl of a pattern like a small shell she had seen on the cover of the Madam's powder case; the fourth bar, seven glances down, a swirling cloud right before the thunder, the angry sky. Her time was contained in the brief moments of associative imagination.

All day long, she followed the design of the bars. The only thing in her mind was the seed growing into her, a child, threatening to betray both of them, growing under the thin cheap red underwear. She was pregnant. Still unrecognizable in others' eyes, but recognizable all too well to other women whose job was to sell their bodies, just like herself. Her breasts had hardened. All signs were there: rejection of food, her body resistant to anything foreign except for the primitive impulse to protect what had become a part of itself.

It had been four months since her last period. Food had become painful for her—anything she ate came out where it came from; as if to replace the basic desire, she had been hungering for exotic things, things she took for granted: tangerines, that sweet and bitter orange fruit only readily available where she grew up. How the mind was easily fooled: the past was a luxury she never thought of now. But now, her body remembered, her body craved for the past, the bitter green fruit that erupted into orange overnight. Even now, as she sat on the stool looking at her face reflected in the water in the bucket in front of her, she could see a vague outline of her mother's face. To anyone here, it was a face of a whore, a low-class whore, named Monkey, the forehead too high and wide, lips too thin, large nostrils at the end of an upturned nose. But to Monkey, it was the face of her mother. People used to tell her that a girl taking after her father would lead a charmed life; Monkey had accepted, that with her mother's face, she must lead the fate of her mother, forever bound to the earth, forever entangled—chained—to the life of a man who was as helpless as she was. As Monkey, too, was now forever bound behind the window, forever bound to the whim of men who entered her not because of her face, not because of love, but because they had extra coins in their wallet to enter a woman, any woman, even a woman as ugly as Monkey.

Monkey had no idea who had fathered the child growing inside of her. She wished that it was a rich man who had slept with her in disguise, but she knew better than to wish. A rich man never visited this whorehouse with the doorway curtained with blue cloth, where nothing remained private. Only men with tired bodies came. Men who hoped to taste women not for who they were, but for what they had between their legs.

She knew all too well the consequences of harboring a child; as prostitutes had to pay for their right to live with their bodies, so they had to pay for the mistake of growing a life. The child born in captivity would be bound to the life of prostitution, her life sealed even before she was born.

She could remember her past, but it all felt like a fleeting dream. The years within the wall were longer than the seasons beyond. But she could not imagine her child, too, living the life she is living. As she sat by herself by the window, she watched the world move without her. Puppets, perhaps, in a play, in which her only role was to watch, and once the play was over, the puppets were put back into boxes backstage, and the audience would go home, except that she had no home to go back to. This was her home. She was a puppet. And home of the life that was growing inside of her.

The bathhouse steamed easily, steam so thick that it hid naked bodies. In this neighborhood, nakedness was nothing shocking; it was a way of life that all neighborhoods all over, known or undiscovered or neglected, had put down as taboo. The proprietor, an old man so old that he was beyond any desire or moral, took money from anyone that passed through the curtain that hung against the door. If he knew which house a girl belonged to, he sent a bill at the end of the month, with an enormous "service fee" added on top: a service, a favor, for serving prostitutes and other people who lived on fringes, who would have had no other place to go to if it weren't for this place. He turned blind eyes to scars and mysterious patches of blisters and botched skins; he turned away from half-rotten limbs and sagging bodies, from dragons and women tattooed on backs. In turn, prostitutes and anyone associated with the body profession could bathe without a second glance and the space people made as prostitutes entered any other bathhouse.

This was a man who kept everyone's secrets. If anything, there were only two things he knew. Not his life, nor his family. He knew his bathhouse, and what it stood for: the money it brought in. Whenever other merchants reminded him that his money was dirty, brought on by bodies, he shrugged his small round shoulders and answered philosophically that money of any kind had to do with the body as commodity: day laborers, fish mongers, farmers, all these money came from limbs extended. *Money was the exchange for time we put in with our body, an exchange for a relief from this world so demanding. It was surer than any intimacy could bring. Lovers changed their minds, children left their parents in their wintering ages, and what remained*, he emphasized, *was money, and nothing else.* He lived by practicality, and that's what Monkey liked about him, though their association was limited to silent nods.

So it went. Taking off her clothes, she glided into the bathroom, suddenly enveloped by steam and gossip and laughter and sighs. Pouring a bucket of warm water on her body, she strained to hear any stories, tangled up stories that had no end nor beginning, as she curled her body around the towel to hide her growing stomach, curled so that it would be encased in folds of her body. Women noticed changes in other bodies. Caution was what she learned during her long seasons here. Even a missed cycle was noticed: *she's been here every day for a couple of months now—she must be missing her period. And you know, that could only mean one thing.*

Bodies of all shapes huddled beyond the steam. Monkey looked around for anyone she could talk to, but finding no familiar face, or with familiar faces but no desire, she began to wash the fold between her thighs first.

Suddenly, the familiar sound of the bathhouse was broken by a shrill laughter. As the sliding door abruptly slammed open, flirtatious laughter only heard from a woman conscious of man erupted.

"Monkey, my dear sister!" the voice bounced against four walls and floor, and then bounced off the ceiling, echoed, erasing the other sound. Watermelon sat next to her proudly.

Monkey hesitated. Quickly picking up the towel that had been huddling in the bucket like an eel, she covered her stomach with it. "I didn't... I didn't know you were planning to bathe this late in the day, Watermelon..." Her heart fluttered like a sparrow, and hoped that echoes of *sister...sister...* overwhelmed what nestled inside of her.

Babbling something, just like the way she had always been, disregarding who was with her, she abruptly turned her back, Watermelon threw the towel over her shoulder, the sound of a wet slap resounding in the bathroom like a challenge that no one dared to take up.

Monkey stared at her back.

"What are you waiting for? Go on, wash my back. Do I have to tell you everything?"

Watermelon's mood changed as quickly as the mood of cats, purring one minute, then clawing in another moment. There was no way to know, unless one was as good at listening and observing like Monkey. And Monkey knew: when a man was around, Watermelon gave away her soul with a glance or laughter. When there was no man, she was bitter and cruel. There was always mystery in her mood. What made her so biting around women, Monkey did not know. Only that she was a woman; that she must be careful.

Rubbing the wash towel against Watermelon's back, Monkey was startled to discover that time, however much Watermelon was conscious of it, tried to avoid it, had left its marks, and continued, even here, away from men's gazes, at the bathhouse, to claw against this woman's body. The skin of her back folding, folded around Monkey's hand, totally submissive to the touch. Catching here and there, Watermelon's skin was no longer resistant, no longer supple and agile, but enfolding, grabbing. She was suddenly reminded of her own mother, far up in North, with her back bent from the moment she opened her eyes to that very moment she blinked herself to sleep. Back curving to see better the place where needles met cloth as she mended the rags that passed as cloth; then late at night, to wash dishes in the bucket full of finger-biting cold water, squatting, examining chipped dishes in the near-dark kitchen. If time was supposed to be gentler to women who spent their days and nights on their backs, their legs spread apart to welcome insertions, then what would it do to a woman's body who had spent all her life with a bent back? An old woman who came to sell them vegetables walked folded at her waist, her chin supported by her stomach. Did her mother look like that now? Monkey shut her eyes to ward off that image; instead, she imagined her unchanged from the day she saw her mother brush her hair, waving at the doorway until she became as invisible as her love for the daughter she sold off. This image was the kindest act she could think to do. It was an act only possible for the daughter she once was, but no longer.

Monkey poured warm water on Watermelon's back, letting water follow the folds, the terrain of this woman who so feared aging, but could not fight.

Only if time would hurry, Monkey prayed, but she also feared that if time did hurry, herded like scattering chickens, it only took her closer and closer to admission, to the fulfillment of the unwilling contract she and the child inside of her made the moment the man—any man, it made no difference now—seeded her. With each passing day, weeks, her breasts seemed to grow as much as her stomach. Her nipples turned dark brown, the dark rings turning bigger, wider, like the spot of the first bleed. They were dark before this, dark even when she first came to this house—what season was it, she wondered. She remembered when she journeyed out of the village that they had started to harvest the meager rouge flowers, her mother's fingers were stained red-orange, which she couldn't get rid of, even after submerging her fingers in ice cold water, even after all the lukewarm baths. She remembered that it was a harvest time because there was not much to harvest, not enough to pay annual taxes. To keep renting the land, they had to come up with money somehow from somewhere. Her mother was bound to the land; she was bound to the debt. And now, Monkey's child, too, would be bound here.

From the faint decrease in temperature in mornings and at night, when her breath became rhythmic tangible blocks of white, she realized that autumn had already passed through, and winter was just outside the fortressed walls of the neighborhood, ready to burst with a signal.

Her worry grew as the child inside of her must be growing, feeding on worry. Someone had talked about it once or
twice in the bathhouse in a hushed tone about how it was until the sixth month the herbs mixed and sold by the vegetable
woman would work; after that, the life lodged permanently
inside a woman. A contract was set: because a woman did not
try to get rid of it, the permission was granted to the life to
come back to this life.

There was no place for a child in this town. Unless the
child was a recently sold girl destined to become a courtesan—a courtesan was, after all an artwork, a product created early on in a woman's life, when a girl before puberty
was chosen based on the promise of great beauty. Or, in some
houses no one talked about, there were said to be girls before
adolescence, some of them as young as six or seven, kept for
the special purpose of satisfying the hunger of men with certain unspoken desires, but these houses were kept quiet by
money for police to turn a blind eye. A child, if born in this
walled city, her birth certificate bound her to this place; she
would never be able to leave this place. She would forever be
bound to the lives of the women here. A child inside of her
had no choice.

Monkey could not allow that.

In the bathhouse, to the keenest of eyes, nothing remained a secret. The first one to notice was the most surpris-
ing of all, the owner of the bathhouse. Usually a man so confined within his property and his thoughts, so bound to the
bathhouse that every time he spoke it was always related to
his business and money, his words surprised Monkey when
one day, the usual nod was not performed. Instead, as Monkey nodded as she parted the curtain and entered the place,
he greeted her with a question.

"Do you have money?"

Startled, Monkey looked up. "Has our Mother not paid the bill for this month?"

Lowering his voice, "That's not what I mean. I mean that," his gaze dropping to Monkey's growing waist, "do you have some nest money to get rid of that?"

Meeting his gaze as it trailed up, then fastening onto his face, she looked deeply into his eyes to see whether she could trust him or not. His gaze was not light, not with the usual indifference, but penetrating, slight curiosity emerging out of compassion that had been hiding in the wrinkled mask of a role he had been playing, as if he, too, like Monkey, had observed, mimicked, acting like the actors with assigned roles. His rough voice tried to mask the gentleness that had been mooring inside of him all these years, perhaps all the reasons he had named that made money the most important thing in his life—the fickle hearts of lovers, the ungrateful children, betrayals—all that made sense to Monkey, that these were all the things he had experienced, etched inside of him so deeply that money outlived every human relationship he ever knew. Monkey, in this instance, glimpsed as much as she understood all his sorrows, choices he had made in his life. She knew she could trust him, after all these years of formal nods, after all the years of roles each had played in order to live, self-effacingly, in this replenishable neighborhood that changed actors as quickly as seasons changed colors.

He nodded, as if he, too, understood all her need to be understood, and beckoned her behind a blue curtain that draped behind him, blue so deep it looked black in the dim interior. He called out to a servant girl to mind the business while he had a chat with a customer about an unpaid bill.

Monkey had seen so many girls disappearing behind this blue curtain. Not until he opened the door behind it did the sunlight make it able to claim back its true color. As anyone else—as all girls had laughed, some more forcibly than others as if they were afraid to reveal secrets they did not dare to reveal, their laughter louder than the coyness of the speaker: he must not be as tough as they say. Look how all these girls he calls in to that room for private "chats about the unpaid bill." And now, she herself stood amidst the sparsely decorated room, with only two threadbare cushions and chipped teacups stacked up, threatening to topple, and a metal kettle steaming on the stove, warming the room.

"So you don't have money. What are you going to do? People are starting to talk quietly, and that would mean that any minute, people will start to talk more loudly than they have been doing."

"What can I do?" Monkey said slowly.

"One thing's for sure: ignoring it doesn't help. Waiting for something to happen doesn't help, because nothing's going to happen unless you do something."

Now, more desperate, she asked what she could do.

"The way I see it, you have three options. One, you can somehow acquire some money, as quickly as you can, and get some herbal packets from the vegetable woman. From what I understand, though, her packets don't work but no one complains about it because if they did, everyone will know that they were pregnant, and were trying to kill babies. Two, you can try to run away, bear a child somewhere by yourself, and leave the child at a temple or one of those foster homes. That's risky, too, because if you run away, you'll have dogs and men chasing after you, and if you get caught, you'll be put into prison. More than likely, they'll feed you to the dogs." He paused, pouring a cup of diluted tea, then another, and placed one in front of Monkey.

Raising three fingers as to emphasize his point, he said slowly, "Three, you can go and stand in the river—it's cold enough now that several hours there, the baby will run down your thighs and down the river. A lot of women die doing that, of course. You don't have much option here without money, if you ask me."

Monkey sat quietly in front of him, listening to his brutal kindness, his truthfulness.

"I don't have much choice here, do I?"

"All three options are risky."

"What do you suggest?"

Eyeing her, he changed the subject and asked her how long she'd been here.

"I've been here... eight years now? I don't remember."

"Well, you belong to that teahouse across from River Entrance Hotel, right? The Madam works you girls from what I hear. She keeps track of everything you eat, every man you sleep with, every bedding you soil. I would guess that with all that debt, and with how much they bought you for, you probably have about three years left to work." He shook his head sadly. "So little time to go... all these eight years, you've managed not to get pregnant, and now... the gods surely are mad in their games. Let me tell you: most girls here have gone into the river and those who came out alive can no longer bear children. There's one or two who've gone to the river several times and they keep going back to the river. Some women are more cursed by gods than others. You look healthy – you may not be able to bear any children after this, but in return, you won't have to ever worry about this, not for three years."

Three more years of worrying, or, her chance of starting her life all over in three years. Three more years. Thousands and hundreds of nights, of countless men going through her. And then, her future. But her child would not have that option. If she had the child, the child would have to be left behind because it would be the property of the brothel. What kind of life would the child have? And when the time arrived, would she be able to leave a child behind?

Yes. There was only one option.

She nodded. She got up.

"I can't offer you anything, even a blessing, Monkey, but I will pray for you that in next life, the gods will be kinder to you. Go—you have decided."

With her bathrobe around her still, and a hand towel crouching in the wooden bucket, she hurriedly left the bathing house. All three gates—North, East, and West—were guarded to keep in prostitutes, but she knew where she could find her way toward the river, the stream fast enough to suck out the life, to give back her own life in exchange for the child's life. The fourth gate was a natural gate, a river deep and wide enough, and a current fast enough that only the desperate attempted to escape by swimming. It was used to ferry masters in anonymously, expensively.

Going through alleys of cluttering houses, of brightly decorated front doors announcing the oncoming changing of the years, passing through the dim dirty backdoors of teahouses, she made her way toward the fourth wall, where women, every morning, made their way, down the ramp to the river bed where boats landed, where women washed their laundry in biting cold water to let the smell of men get carried away downstream to another part of the world, where women and girls' fingers turned bright red, then chapped, bleeding all during winter, the coldness of water reopening cracks bigger and bigger until their hands were chapped like dried land. She knew her way down there because it was one of her jobs, because she was the lowest in the hierarchy, because men came to Watermelon for smoothness, but came to Monkey for one thing, which was not for her hands.

This early in the afternoon, no woman washed, for only the time between breakfast and lunch was open for washing before they had to prepare for the night—to oil down their own, or for laundresses, someone else's hair, to whiten napes, to rouge lips, to go to dance or music lessons, if they were lucky enough to be a courtesan. And no boat dared to come in this bright sunlight. During the daytime, the neighborhood was a women's town, where women moved around freely, because they owned it for a few hours. At night, it was suddenly bulging with men, men from all different kinds of lives, men who took on different names, men who suddenly became single, though their wives were asleep by themselves somewhere outside the walls, where people went about their days and died, not bound to fate.

The river was wide and fast, ground covered in sharpened rocks. That was why no one had attempted to guard the fourth wall – the very place Monkey stood. No one attempted to escape by swimming because if they did, their clothes would suck up all the water, drag them to the bottom, where rocks sharp as knives waited to pierce; if they did manage to keep their heads up, the current was too strong for them to swim straight. It would carry them so quickly, so swiftly and effortlessly, to the waterfall waiting only a few paces down. People came here to die. And only a few bodies turned up; once in a while, a bloated corpse was fished out when an arm or a leg got trapped between sharp rocks, so sharp that their bodies, if time had not already feasted upon it, were battered unrecognizable by the river itself.

Monkey walked along the small landing and reached the low bushes overhanging the river. Grabbing the thickest branch, she lowered herself slowly, toes first, toes flinching reflexively, shying away from the bitter cold. Then her ankles, slowly, the shock of cold making the body revolt away from the water automatically, as if to save itself. Even before her ankles were submerged, she could feel her stomach, her breasts, slowly losing warmth, her head exploding in pain. Her teeth chattered staccato against each other; when her soles touched the ground, blood gushed out, then stopped. Still, she kept on, submerging herself to her knees, then kneeling, she plunged

herself to her stomach. The robe pasted around her, the outline of her stomach more accentuated, more pronounced; the
water kept tugging at her, tugging, threatening to grab her
whole body, her hands shaking against the branch, against
itself, wanting to hold on, yet not to. The river threatened to
carry her downstream, like all those women who had disappeared suddenly, who had disappeared from teahouses and
bathhouses, who had been swallowed up by this very river to
be carried away somewhere downstream, their faces anonymous, their shame for all to see, their bodies so far away from
where they originated, alone.

Every time the coldness overtook her senses, every time
her mind threatened to shut itself off, she tried to imagine
her way back to the village three years from now, when all the
debts she'd never seen but believed—if not for some kind of
meaning to her own life, then for her parents—were paid off,
her life a clean slate. Shedding the past one by one, year by
year, slowly and surely as she made her way back. She thought
of that, she tried to think of the paths she would need to take,
as coldness engulfed her mind, her grip, as the freezing water
all around her threatened to overtake her, and tried to make
her forget why she was there. It was her body she was trying
to save, her own life, not the life inside her, that life that had
wormed its way, dug on, and housed itself inside of her. Her
knees no longer felt razored; her body began to spasm un-
controllably, jerked into unconscious movements, a puppet
jerked with the rhythm of the strong current.

Even after the body gave up shivering, after the body
gave up trying to keep itself warm, fingers losing sensation,
even after the blood began to concentrate only on the heart,
abandoning limbs; even after fingers turned a blue so deep it
almost looked like they should not belong to the breathing
body, but to a body that the soul had already rejected, she
kept kneeling, praying to the only god she knew—the god

she did not know the name of—she prayed for the life inside of her to reject her, to reject the possibility of life, so that Monkey could live for another three years, so that she could retrace the path she had taken eight years ago, and see the mountain range that turned furious orange every fall, where orange blossoms, turning into paste in her mother's hands, could make their way down the mountain to towns all over this land, so that the child would not have to live her life, as much as her mother didn't want Monkey to live her life. Because she loved the child growing inside of her, because she loved it enough, Monkey had no choice except to let this child go. She prayed. She prayed as she stood in the river.

But the god did not hear her prayer. The life inside of her resisted, fought, clawed into the interior of the womb, and claimed its life as its own, not the body it had temporally housed itself in. Her stomach grew and grew until the contraction came months later, and after hours of pain, the baby slid down, took her first breath, and cried and wailed. The only thing Monkey could do was to reach over and unscrew the case. Dabbing her smallest finger, she dabbed the rouge on her fingertip, the rouge the color of the orange blossom, and, looking at the face of her girl, her baby, she tapped the crying lips with the rouge. And Monkey cried, knowing her own child's life was done for already, fated, limited, and without escape from this very moment on.

confession

In darkness, space contracts, and we must make an uncertain contract with it in order to save ourselves from breaking. (As I sit here, I am no longer sure of who I am. I am forgetting who I was before all this happened; I am forgetting myself.) It was perhaps a week ago, or maybe a month ago, I am no longer sure, when they came to my house and told me of the arrest, and I stood there with all the gestures of what I was doing moments ago held in one pose, doubting my own ears. I told them there must've been some mistake, that they must have gotten the house wrong, but the police said that they were never wrong. He said I must come with him. They work for Americans, they said, and America is always right. It is just. It is all knowing. What saves us in this darkness is not the memory of outside, but the past, these events that we have experienced, revised every moment at the whim of our emotions. What saves us is not what has been locked in this cell, but what is far removed from here.

(The war. How long ago it was. We were hungry for such a long time and men kept disappearing, drafted at all hours. The voice in the radio kept telling us that we were winning, that we destroyed this convoy in the southern sea, we destroyed that fleet of B29s with Special Force airplanes slamming themselves against the flying fortress. The entire nation was tired, constantly jerked awake two, three times a night, running away from the bombs to the shelters, always losing a neighbor, a child, a friend, on the way. How we would come out of the shelters, bewildered, tired, only to find our homes obliterated, and how we hated the Americans. How we so wanted to kill them. The war ended abruptly, we were told to pack up everything and hide in the mountains because the Americans were coming, because they would rape all women, that they would castrate men as they would a pig. And they did come. But they did not rape; they did not castrate. We sighed in relief; we waited for our men to come home.)

How long can a person last in the darkness?

For as long as their mercy lasts.

How long can a body hold on to a soul, or a soul stay in the body before they part from each other like separating lovers, their farewells brief and formal after a long, drawn-out regret?

As long as they will it. The definition of imprisonment is that your life no longer is yours to control, your body theirs. Your mind theirs. They can revise your past, make you into the vision of who they think you are.

How long can a person last in the silence of his own past?

As long as silence is not broken by the confession.

(I am innocent. I have not done anything. Only if they tell me what it is I have done. If only they will tell me my crime then can I think of what I might have done.)

A week ago, I was standing in the field, blinded by the sun, but back then, the sun was a blessing, a curse, something we took for granted until something happened. A week ago, they knocked on the door as I was cooking supper, the usual supper of gruel and simple vegetables, seasoned with spring weeds. My daughter sat near the fire, kneading her sore muscles like we do with sticky rice on festival days, kneading out tiredness like we pound out air from the dough. When the knock came, my daughter grumbled, then slowly opened the door to let in the cold air and the men from the police station, all the men familiar to us. They said that they needed to take me away; they said that a war criminal had confessed, and mine was one of the names she confessed. My hands stopped all the movements, and I only listened, in a removed way like you would listen to a far away cry of a child in a neighborhood late at night.

The men told us that they were sorry, but they never made mistakes; they had all the proof.

The proof, what is it? I demanded.

A woman—we can't tell you her name—said, under oath, that you, with five other women, killed a man. Yes, that is enough for now, they said. And they held my arms, my daughter bawled and clung to the policeman's leg, crying and begging, until a neighbor came and dragged her away. They led me through the dark village filled with my daughter's wail to the darkened cell. They told me to wait here until they came to get me to confess. And even in the cell, I heard my daughter crying.

Do not think of the sun. Do not think of what is outside

the door. Do not think of the life you have left behind, people you have left behind. Do not think of where you are.

The sun does not miss you. What is immediately outside of the door is interrogation. When they single you out, that is when they take you away to *that* room, to ask about all the crimes you did not commit. The life outside goes on without you; people fall in love, they fall out of love, they die in their beds or on fields, they embrace each other without thinking about you. And where you are, this is the only place you can be.

Think instead of your past.

(Think of any past. Think of your daughters, the one waiting for you, and the one you killed. Think of anything but where you are.)

(My husband. How he didn't want to go to the war. We had been joking, he was too old; he was too frail, and a father besides and no one drafted a father. But the notice came. A crippled boy, the one the government didn't want because one of his legs was shorter than the other half, brought the notice, *congratulations, you have been drafted to serve His Majesty The Emperor and Our Imperial Motherland,* and as he had been taught, my husband thanked him, and said that he would sacrifice his body and soul and die for the nation. The paper the color of blood. They gave us three days. Three days to say good-bye, three days of a lifetime, and we spent it, the four of us, curled up together.)

Day or night, I am no longer sure. I know the afternoon starts when they open the slot and throw in food, and all of us rattle our chains, each in our corners, our pieces of miracle, to circle around the food like once-tamed dogs now gone wild. And the night starts when they throw in food, "dinner" they call it, though it is the same food they throw in for lunch.

(The morning he left for the war, he sat and watched our two girls sleeping. And I watched him. That's how I remember him, so tender, the way he always was, stroking their cheeks again and again. The time stopped. The morning light stood still, and I watched him, from the doorway, wishing for this moment to last, for the world to end, now, so that I could remember him, just like this. This is how I remember him still.)

I am no longer sure of how many of us there are. It could be five. It could be four. When one of us is taken outside, I am not sure if it is the same person who comes back; it may be a new person, or a person who was taken but is no longer the same. Only filth, the stench from our bodies—the sour smell of weeks-old sweat. And stench from our waste. And sometimes, I smell death; it is the smell of the monthly fluid, but stronger, more persistent, the kind of smell that can only be described as the smell of death. I know death by how I itch more; fleas have ways of detecting death before the owner of the body. They climb up to the face, then depart in search for warm kinetic bodies. And as soon as fleas migrate to us, the rattle of chains becomes more frequent as we scratch frantically from the sudden overpopulation of fleas.

(*Promise me you'll look after our children, don't let anything happen to them.* The voice in the dark. I look away.)

We try not to talk about who we are here amongst us because inevitably, stories heard in the darkness have ways of being used against you. Nothing is safe, not ourselves from each other. That's how things were before the war, when the socialists and communists disappeared with the night, and we would find their bodies, their bones broken, dead, thrown out on the streets like dead dogs in the morning. We heard of their checkered past, and that's how they were punished. Instead, I tell myself stories of the past, to remind myself of who I am, before my past is erased by confusion, before they take away my past.

(Was it my older daughter who woke me up that night when the siren began to pierce through the dark? Or was it the earth shaking, trembling, making its tremor felt even on the second floor where we slept? The rhythmic shake of the house, of the city itself, like the staccato and practiced drum beats of jazz that had been banned when the war started? Everything was dark, windows covered with old newspapers and thick paper so that the city could disappear into the night, so that no light could be seen for the enemy to attack. Then something thunderous struck, with sirens going off stronger, and suddenly all our windows became a furious red, as if there were red waves rolling outside. I held the younger daughter's hand, told the older daughter to grab the bag, and we ran through burning streets and buildings spitting out people, all screaming and panicking. We ran and ran. The bomb shelter could be reached with no more than three minutes running on a quiet, practice day. No one seemed to care about the burning houses that night—all these hours and days of women practicing, relaying water buckets to put out fire—no one seemed to care or remembered. We ran along with the sea of people, all heading toward the bomb shelter. The siren blared out of speakers, then suddenly went quiet. Only the cracking sounds of wood splitting, tongues of fire sneaking into spaces not visible to the naked eye, sounds of people yelling and pushing to get ahead of each other; babies crying. The sky had turned into frantic fireworks, though it was still early in the spring. With a whistling sound, a bomb fell behind us, then another ahead, a third to the east. The earth trembled all around, rumbling, trembling, as if we were in the stomach of a hungry monster that had swallowed us. We threw ourselves into the shelter where so many people squatted, scared, full to the doorway. *Close the door*, someone yelled. And that's when I realized that my elder daughter was nowhere in sight.)

The door opens. The light blinds us, and we raise our chained arms to shield our eyes from the intrusion. Handcuffs rattle from our separate corners. They go around, one by one, making sure that we are still alive, slapping us awake, slapping us to make sure we still feel the pain. Today, everyone is still alive. They ask if we have mended our ways.

I didn't do anything, let me out, I'm innocent, someone shakes her chains and yells, though her voice is shaky and unsure, as if she has nearly forgotten how to speak in the darkness.

We know what you did. That's why you're here. We never make mistakes, a man says in a gentle voice. He wears a dark uniform, blending into the dark. *You know what you did*, the man in a dark uniform repeats himself. He then looks around, his face scanning us one by one, smiling and nodding as our eyes meet, as his eyes meet mine.

How are you holding up? Are you ready to talk to me? he asks me gently as he kneels in front of me, our eyes never detaching themselves from each other.

I nod once, then look down, my wrists still held high by the chain.

Are you ready to confess? he lifts my chin with his damp hand. Our eyes meet.

What is there to confess? I say. *I don't know why I'm here. I miss my family. I want to go home. What did I do? Just tell me*

what I did, then I can tell you all you want to hear, I scream
out in desperation.
  You know what you've done, he says.
  A woman stands up. She says that she is ready to talk.

(And it's my fault. I told my elder daughter to grab the
bag. I didn't hold her hand. All through the night, I held my
younger daughter close to me. I prayed that my elder daughter
made her way to another shelter, anywhere. I waited for the
bombings to stop. I prayed for the morning to come. As soon
as it was safe, I pushed the steel door open, I left the younger
daughter with a neighbor, and I ran, I ran though the rubble
that wouldn't let me run. I ran toward the buildings, through
the buildings, to look for the red jacket that she was wearing. I push people, grab girls with red jackets, I push the red
debris to unearth her from under the still smothering woods.
My daughter. I must search for my girl, my daughter, the one
who looked more like my husband. Where was she? Diving
into the charred houses, pushing the still-hot soot aside, and I
would have pushed aside the whole city, swallowed the whole
city to drain it, to look for her. I shouted something, to someone, anyone, to go find someone, anyone, anyone to drag off
this rubble, to find a little girl who might be hiding amidst
the weight. *Mama, I'm here!* I expected her to say anytime,
jumping out of the unburned house or coming around the
corner, the girl who liked to hide, mutating her body into the
shape of whatever she could hide into or under, the unmade
blanket strewn carelessly after a night's sleep, still holding the
warmth of the dreams and nightmares, one time in the bottom drawer of an unused chest. Anywhere but the house. No,
not the house. The neighborhood men and women came out
to look for her, but they were searching for their own missing as well; women came by with rationed tea that was too
bitter. After two weeks of sleepless nights and days, search-

ing for her, men pushing away the burnt beams, the collapsed bomb shelters, they brought back a red jacket with her identification tag sewn on and the bag. *Her body crumbled to our touch, these were the only things we could save.*)

She does not come back. Not after supper. Not after lunch. She is gone, perhaps confessing all that she did, all that she did not do. Perhaps naming us as her accomplices. It does not matter any more. I do not know what silent dialogue she had been carrying on while she was amongst us; I do not know what inner recollections brought her to that confession. But any minute now, we knew that something may happen to all of us; she may say who or what, embellishing her stories, truth or lies, it does not matter, if disfigured into monstrous shape. We could no longer tell where our own stories ended, and where others' stories started.

We must be here because of the Americans, someone mutters. Gasps come out, here and there; a gasp escapes from me. *The American... the American...* voices chatter.
How could I forget.
The American.
Something happens. A light, a truth that worms out of its dark hiding place like a worm hiding in the core of the apple, emerging into the light, wriggling its body toward the light. The American, yes. Someone must have found out about the American.

(One day, near the end of the war, I was on the field. The sky was beautiful, so clear, that for a fraction of a second, I forgot about the war, about the hardship, and it was as if I were back in the time before the war, only four of us, my husband, my daughters. Not the half of what we are now. I thought of the day when my husband might walk through the door, the day when everything would be made all right, and even our dead daughter would come back, having stayed at the orphanage. That's when I saw a lone silver plane wavering through the sky with a trail of two columns of black smoke, and suddenly losing balance, falling from the sky. I don't know where the plane crashed, but I saw one black dot jumping out of the plane, falling quickly, then a white parachute opening up like a mushroom. The dot came closer and closer to the ground. I ran toward where it might land. By the time I got to the tree, where the American-devil hung from the branch, the entire village had come out with weapons in our hands: hoes, pitch-forks, machetes, rusty swords. The policeman—the same one as the one who arrested me—had told us that when Americans came, we had to stab them, just like we've been training to do, stab them in their stomachs so that they'd suffer, so that they'd curse the day they were born.)

On one break of the light, they come to get me. They tell me that a witness named me as one of the few who murdered. They unchain me, not unkindly, but not painfully, not the way they would treat the already condemned. I stumble, my first steps in so many days. How long have I been here, I ask weakly, my throat constricting from thirst, from lack of use. They tell me two weeks, no, ten days, this is my eleventh day.

(Is the American what they want to hear?)

Your daughter's been worried, she comes every day and pesters us. Cute kid. Don't worry, they say, *we give her chocolates the GIs give us,* they say.

I shake my head as they help me walk through the dark and dirty hallway, both sides with doors that seem to contain many lives inside, just like the one I have left behind. We slowly walk through the short hall, up the narrow and steep stairs that threatened to topple me if it weren't for the men behind me, if it weren't for my arms holding on to both walls as we walk up. I think of my daughter. I think of my husband. I think of the day when the American came falling from the sky.

When we get to the top floor, they become different. They shove me into a bare room that contains only a stool, a desk, and chairs. Some men are already perched there like owls, their faces betraying no emotion that I can decipher.

We know that you were there where the American aviator landed on our village, one of them says in a practiced voice, as if I am no longer a woman they have seen but already one of the enemy.

I shake my head, my voice caught suddenly dry, like morning sickness. But nothing comes out.

We have witnesses, they have told us, all of them, that they saw you there, another one says.

I shake my head again. I will my throat to open, to tell the only truth I know. Finally, my mouth opens, and the weak words dribble out, one by one, as if I am spitting out rocks stuffed in my mouth, *I do not know what you are talking about.*

(The American-devil aviator was blond, big, his uniforms tattered, and he was trying to untangle himself from the parachute. He was yelling something, but he spoke in the tongue of the devil, of the beast, and we were scared.)

The pen scratches furiously against a parchment, filling the silence between us.

We have sworn witnesses all saying that on a Sunday past July, Lieutenant Colonel James Morse III of the American Air Force's plane crashed, and he survived. He was murdered by you.

No, no, I do not know what you are talking about, I almost shout back, but even this shout comes out as whispers.

I am no longer sure of what is real, what was real, or who I am.

We have sworn witnesses before the court of law that several people saw you with a sword, and you delivered the fatal blow that killed him.

I don't even own a sword, I say, *everything I owned burned down the day the Americans bombed the city. I came to the village with what I had on and my youngest daughter.* But my words are not at all strong; they are weak. Weaker than my body.

(Look how big he is; look how hairy he is. And still defiant. Look how he kept chewing and chewing, looking down on us from his height. The police finally came as we all circled him like hungry dogs. They chained him and dragged him through the village, circling again and again, and the angry buzz grew louder and louder until the chants became clear: *kill the American-devil, kill the American-devil.*)

And is it not true, another starts, *you tried to cover up your crime by burying the said Lieutenant Colonel?*

I did him no harm. I wasn't the only one there. The entire village was out. I wasn't the only one. I don't own a sword. I say as I see the dead body, the unmoving body of the American, *Je-i-mu-su Mo-su,* the enemy with a name, the former enemy, a man. A dead man.

(I couldn't hold it anymore, we couldn't hold it, all the nights of bombardment, all the deaths of our sons and husbands and fathers, all the things no one should endure. My daughter in her red coat, who died without leaving a body behind. My husband who didn't want to go to war. I knew then: it was him up in the sky that night. He came and dropped the bomb. He killed my daughter. It's his fault. We mobbed in; we circled him, and once we were done, he stumbled, then fell, his matted and bunched hair falling with him, and for a second, he did not look like a man anymore but a rag, a scarecrow, a tattered cloth.)

They thrust a photo at me: a young man with a boyish grin, in a uniform.

Another photo: he stands with his family—his parents, his two sisters.

And the sudden dawning, as if things finally make sense, and I am no longer blinded by light, by shock, but I can see now.

(He lay on the ground, still, and I kicked him. And I remember: he uttered a beastly sound the moment my foot made its contact with the body. The ground was ready for planting, and we bore down on it with all our might to bury the secret that must not be seen by anyone. We walked with a bundle amongst us, heavy and sodden from the blood of the American devil. The ground was frozen and we thrust the bundle as soon as we opened the earth, enough to bury the American head first. And as soon as the secret was safely in ground, we prayed for the earth not to betray us. We prayed, and we went home, to our separate homes. And we forgot all about it, with the surrender, with the war lost, with the new world that came when we were vanquished.)

I shake my head. I nod. I shake my head, then nod over and over to their questions until that is the only gesture I know how to make, but I am no longer sure of my own version of the story. Words blur, time contracts, and I do not know whose past they are talking about.

By the time they are through with questioning, I no longer know who I am.

(Maybe I really did kill the American. Maybe my kick was what killed him. They say the sword cut killed him, but who is to stay that a kick can't be as deadly as a sword?)

(No, it never happened the way they said it happened.)

(Yes it did. No, what I remember is the truth.)

They feed us.

(Can I really go back to the sun, to the light, if I only say yes?)

I can almost see the American, still alive between our kicks, screaming as we mobbed him to pieces, as blood splatters, and we smear our hands with the warm blood. I can almost see it; I feel the blood, warm and slimy liquid trailing down my thighs like snails trailing on flesh. I can almost believe it.

(Is this what really happened?)

A woman coughs in the dark corner. Another mutters a prayer of hope. Of salvation. Of deliverance. For my daughter. What is true in the sunlight is no longer visible, no longer visible in the darkness.

(I am done for.)

A woman coughs in the dark corner. Another mutters a prayer of hope.

(And is this not a dream? A woman coughs, but only in a dream; another mutters a prayer, but is this really a dream?)

I am done for in the darkness, and a woman coughs a dark prayer into the corner of hope.

(A prayer: the light: the darkness. Am I done for?)

how we touch the ground, how we touch

A s usual, another season of betrayal must follow the harvest.

During the harvest, we are safe. On the field, we whisper half a phrase and hum fragmented sounds of words amongst us, messages of the Carpenter-Son hidden in broken phrases of weather and harvest. We bend our backs to cut the stalks, huddling as close to the ground as we can, but not falling. Even the strongest of us bow our backs as low as the translucent stalks of rice, golden skeletons bowing with the autumn bounty. Cutting the fistful of stalks in the rhythm of gravity, hoe against the bundle, fist around the bunch, we gather this year's harvest slowly. Then, after the harvest, we will turn the earth upside down to dig out roots that have clawed their way down, deep into the soil. But until then, we drag the harvest time out as long as we can, and time becomes elastic, easily moldable in our hands.

The harvest is good this year, and because of that our season of betrayal follows immediately afterward.

All hours are hours of apostates for us who must live through the season of betrayal. All hours are a litany of passion, though our passions are invisible, less obvious than those of the Carpenter-Son. In this hour of apostates, in the field, all of us are alike: men take on the slender napes of women, bobbing up and down with the northern wind that signals the arrival of autumn, and women take on tree-like stumps for legs because we are so near to the ground, because our days are measured by how close we can get to the ground without falling. As we rhythmically cut down the harvest, the Elder starts a hymn, a chant unlike the one Domu-niku had taught us, but the one we have cut out from the original to bury the message into songs more familiar to us. The Elder sings of the Paraiso, of the Carpenter-Son, the promised land and of ourselves, who amongst us will carry on the season of betrayal. And who amongst us must die. It is decided: this season, the Elder will die because De-us our Father has given permission, to him and his family. We will carry it out, we sing out. The Elder sings in praise of De-us, in praise of the sun and the rain that give, that destroy whatever tries to ground itself to earth, he sings of De-us and His mysterious way, of the sweet revelation, the little lamb, lamb, of the Paraiso, yes, the Paraiso.

Abruptly, his song turns into a hushed hum of one note, suspended like the body of the faithful, as we hear the procession of our landlord, steps and grunts of horses on the mud road, that ground that sounds softer than it really is, and no one can say that the mud is soft when they have been thrown into a hole filled with mud. The cold kills; the slow oozing of mud clogs the pores until the flesh begs off, when the flesh begs off the soul it encases. And we have all done that. We have betrayed De-us in those moments when we were encased in mud, confessing the crime of believing Him.

The Third Elder sings one note, and one note only, as his face masks into empty indifference, as our faces take on the faces of the apostates.

We call it the season of betrayal. They call it cleansing. It is a law, they tell us, why do you only want one god when there are so many amongst us. Why believe in a god when so many of you have fallen, and He still remains quiet to your prayers? They tell us many things as they line us up and tell us to step on the face of our Beloved, and we, one by one, step on the face, step on the face of the Carpenter-Son and His mother, Maria of the miracle, Maria of the Stabat Mater. After each harvest, we line up one after another, the procession of all the apostates before us, all the apostates that will come after us, even after our bodies have been rooted to the earth, after our bodies become another element to feed the bodies after us. We step on their faces to prove we do not love Them, though we do. Our hearts break. It has been going on for twelve years, ever since Domu-niku fell.

The hours of the apostates started out one day when a man with sky in his eyes appeared in front of us from the cave by the edge of our village. He spoke our tongue in fragments, but when he spoke, he spoke of the Land, of De-us. In his halting tongue, he pointed at his tattered sparrow-brown robe, said, *Domu. Niku.* Domu-niku, we called him. He spoke of a world better than this one, about a world where hunger was kept at bay, where the tilling of earth was as forbidden as the utterance of the real name of gentle Father in this world. De-us. Domu-niku told us, he told us many things and we drank his words greedily as if we were thirsty, as if we never knew we were thirsty until we drank the first word, and we became thirstier and thirstier the more we heard him talk. See, he told us, your hands are not used properly. See, he told me as he gently cupped my hands with his, see how your palms are like slightly eroded maps with so many rivers running through? How they have been telling you that your palms are a map of your life, the life you must live? Press them together, like this, like this, he said as he pressed his hands together and pressed my hands as if he were pressing a flower between pages to be kept, there, your life disappears. This is the life you are meant to have, a life in prayer. He gently pulled me into his arms, and he smelled of a cow, a pig, something so earthbound that if it were another man, I would have thought that he could never be a man carrying the words of De-us.

Pray, and De-us will respond.

Pray so that the land will parch, cracks opening for the rain that would never come; pray so that the water will submerge the land, so that people will be covered in boils and scabs, so that the faithless will die and the Gates of Paraiso will open up to spit out winged men. Pray so that we can be delivered to the arms of De-us.

Pray so that our palms will erase all the foredoomed lives we must live; pray so hard that our palms will blister from the pressure.

Only then will the Man-Bird listen, only when all the faithfuls' palms are bleeding like the hands of the Carpenter-Son, the hands of the holy as He bled from His hands in order to purify the land.

But not until then.

They came at night and caught Domu-niku with three of us. One of us betrayed us though we do not know who. When

three of the villagers were bound together in the shape of a rosary, their torsos and strong arms bound, when they whipped
them forward up the mountain as we followed, slowly, when
they stood at the mouth of the volcano mountain, Domu-niku
cried out once, then twice. They did not hold him down; they
only asked that he watch, and we watched him as we watched
with these three martyrs. *All you have to do is to renounce your
faith, and you will save these people,* a voice emerged out of
the forest as if it was not a voice of a man but the sky itself,
but if you don't, then they will have to die for your faith. They
first kicked the old Elder into the broiling mouth, and held
the next-in-chain by the lip; the Elder bobbed up and down
midair, unable to go down, unable to go up, burning, but not
burning. The Elder cried out the name of De-us, only to be
erased by the roar of the volcano. *Foreigner, your god tells you
not to kill, but you are killing them.* Domu-niku, unable to
run toward them nor run away, kneeled and turned to us for
prayers, but we did not offer him prayer or consolation. We
just looked down, making ourselves unnoticeable. We could
be next, but we did not tell Domu-niku that we feared dying,
we feared that we have not seen De-us as Domu-niku has, but
we believed him. We believe him so that we can dream of a
better world. And mostly, we feared that after all the prayers,
all the praises and all the dead bodies, we feared not finding
De-us when we crossed over to the other side, that all our
prayers were made in vain.

The elder's rope burned. He fell into the mountain, disappeared. The next one in the chain hanged from the lip of
the mountain, his scream as loud as the boar fighting back
during the hunt. The woman at the end of the rosary jerked
forward, and they held her tight, Domu-niku's refusal held
her to the top, she was at the mercy of one word, but it was
only a mere word. *It's your last chance, Christian man—say
you will renounce, and you're saving these lives.* Domu-niku

kept shaking and praying, pressing his palms together, praying for guidance, for mercy, God, *God why have you forsaken
me at this time of need, I am only human, God, please, tell me
what to do*, and he raised his arms toward the sky, kneeling on
the ground, digging deep into the sand. He raised his arms
upward, his palms still pressed together.

Last chance—where's your god when you need him?

God, Domu-niku shouted, *God, what can I do?* His hands
still held in the form of a prayer, he yelled, his face upturned
to the sky, and not even a bird replied.

The voice, in a startlingly sad tone, almost a wail of a
gull's before the storm, crooned out of the trees, *Well, so be
it. I'm sorry.*

The last bead of rosary disappeared into the volcano; they
all looked at the place where the three of us fell. They turned
to us. We kept our eyes to the ground.

Still kneeling, Domu-niku's hands flew apart, some force
greater than the one in his heart, pried his hands apart. Palms
orphaned from each other. He clawed, he would have clawed
out the sun, the eye of De-us, if he could have. Veins grew
on his upturned arms, fists grew at the end of his upturned
arms.

He collapsed to the ground; he fell to the ground and
cried.

He became the first to fall.

Domu-niku the apostate.

He now carries the branded cross on his face, though
he is no longer the Domu-niku who stood straight, his legs
firm on the ground as he taught us about Paraiso, of the Carpenter-Son, his Mother, the Domu-niku who had held my
hands, the Domu-niku who had traveled three years across
the ocean in order to spread the words of De-us. He is of the
outcast, orphaned from his Father, Ada-mu outcast from

Paraiso, orphaned and left to live in a country so far away from the origin of his faith.

Domu-niku the man, a mere fallen man who has thrown away the frock he had arrived in and has taken on new clothes, a new name, and many new gods. He no longer holds our hands in the dark night, listening to our confessions; he no longer talks of his Paraiso, the Land kept behind his shut mouth, and now, he talks of the starry sky and of the lands we have never seen nor believed to exist.

He became the first fallen one, and our season of betrayal began that year.

And I hold on, as we all do, on to the words of Domu-niku, as we cup our hands around the rice husks, the golden husks standing out radiant as Domu-niku said about the ray of God and the Beloved, and each harvest, we hold God in our hands, our private God, our own because Domu-niku said that he is in our hearts, because He is the only thing that is ours, because the land is not ours and our lives not our own. The husks, brilliant, as our love for Him. Then clouds cover the sun, always at our moments of illumination, and the golden husk returns to this ordinary earthiness, the rice that measures our worth, and our lives that have no meaning.

De-us the god of the golden husk has been silent all these times.

We pray in vain, late at night, when no one is around, when it is only the apostates awake, uttering our prayers into holes in houses where no one can hear. We carry our faith as all apostates do, and we call it the hours of apostates. And for apostates, all hours are hours of apostates. Our lives are measured by all these hours we must live as apostates.

And this year, at the late hour before the gathering of harvest, a week ago, our Elder gathered us, because we no longer have Domu-niku to call us, because the season of betrayal will start soon. He said that he had a dream, a dream so beautiful that if what he saw was Paraiso, he'd rather be there than where he was. *Maria the mother was there, the Carpenter-Son, and all the twenty-six martyrs who died, they told me that it is my turn to be the apostle. He told me that my job is done, and I can do nothing more. In the dream, He lifted my robe and touched my cross, and He unrobed his tattered robe, one for each season of betrayal. I have cut myself deep, and I carry twelve lines to show, the black welts as thick as worms,* twelve fierce worms wiggled vertically as he breathed hard, *it is my turn,* they told me, *I no longer have to step on Their faces. I have been carrying the weight of our burden.* His wife and daughter clasped their hands together in prayer.

You are now the leader, he turned to me. *You are now the Elder; you must lead these children as I have done, hiding our faith, hiding who we truly are so that you can deliver them to Paraiso. Your path will be hard, but remember that it is not as hard as the Carpenter-Son. You know what you must do.*

I have been chosen.

The harvest has been good. We will not eat what we have worked hard at. The earth itself is full of bounty, golden and already luxurious before it must sleep during winter in order to repeat the cycle all over again. The harvest has been good. And the season of betrayal will start soon. It has been like this for twelve years now. They test us, to see that we do not believe in De-us.

We go to the temple, as we always have done. We stand in the line with our eyes downcast. The former Elder is the only one who looks straight at them. At Domu-niku, who stands with his back stooped, down to our heights, not looking at anyone. Domu-niku who is no longer Domu-niku; who now has a new name, new wife, and new role. The line crawls forward as one by one, we step on the faces of Maria and the Carpenter-Son. It is quiet, though our hearts are breaking inside, though we are wailing as we step on the faces of our Beloved. And suddenly. The Elder calmly steps away from the line. His wife and daughter step away from the line with him. He announces that he cannot lie, no matter what, not anymore, not ever. The Elder says that he is too tired to live the life of a lie, an apostate, and he is an apostle, he has been the apostle who has had to live as an apostate. Taken by surprise, they ask him kindly what he means. Domu-niku does not look at the Elder.

And the Elder recites what all of us hope to recite openly, the names of De-us, the Carpenter-Son, the glorious triangle of mysteries; he pours forth the forbidden stories and glories of De-us. Paraiso, Paraiso, the Elder sings, Deus, deus, deus, he sings, and his daughter and wife join him, their voices weaving into a triangle of songs in the fall sky of the harvested earth.

Do you understand what you are doing, Domu-niku asks quietly, *do you understand what they'd do to you once they know you are believer of a foreign heathen god?*

The trinity of voices do not quiet, but insistently push themselves forward to their end. They are bound there. They tell us we must watch as a punishment for harboring these "Christians," they tell us that in order that we will not protect any more of these people, we must participate in the punishment. They say that they'll tell us what, later, what we have to do. We already know what we must do.

They coax him, holding his daughter and his wife, telling him that if he does not renounce De-us, they will have to make him submit. He shakes his head with a smile, *See how foolish you are. De-us is closer than you think, He stands here, with me, and understands that I can no longer lie, even if I wanted to.*

They, too, shake their heads, *Do you understand what you are saying, this is your daughter and wife.*

And the Elder stands firm in his faith, in his conviction, telling them that He does not allow His children to take their own lives, but if He gives permission, we can leave. And He has given the permission, glory and mercy.

They do not touch him. But Domu-niku steps up in the front, binds the daughter and wife. They pour cold water on them, Domu-niku jabs a dull knife under their fingernails, they scream, they scream, they pray and call out the names of De-us, and the louder their screams, the more joyously and loudly the Elder sings of Paraiso and of De-us, and we watch with our closed faces. Domu-niku's face is closed as ours as he jabs the knife one by one, twenty in total; he keeps his eyes away as he slices off their noses and ears, slowly. They put the former Elder into a bamboo cage and make him watch.

And it does not end. Domu-niku makes the daughter and the wife dig two holes deep enough and wide enough so that a body can sit in each; the Elder sings from the cage like a domesticated finch. He stays like that for a week while the wife and the daughter sit tied to the tree with their faces branded with burns in the shape of a cross. He watches his wife and daughter poked around with hot rods while he sings of Paraiso, never once wavering in his resolution. And we watch with him. We watch as Domu-niku stares at the ground.

Finally, they make the daughter and wife sit in the holes so that the Elder can throw the dug earth back around and they make him stomp on freshly dug earthen holes and he stomps wildly, almost a dance, a passionate dance. Two tired heads poke out of the ground as if someone had gently placed two beheaded heads on the ground. They hand the Elder a rusty saw taken out of someone's shed and command him to saw off their heads.

It's because of your foolish faith, they yell, *you don't have to kill your daughter and wife. We hate to do this, we do, you understand, we never want to harm you people.*

The Elder's head pops up and down as if his head is held only by thin skin, as if it is his head that is getting sawn off with a rusty saw. And he sings and sings, his voice breaks, cracking, so much like Domu-niku's that day, anguished, breaking. Domu-niku wailed out questions; the Elder wails out songs of De-us. We stare at the ground, unyielding ground. The Elder sings and, following the rhythm of the saw, he begins to saw off his daughter's head, and the wife joins him, singing joyously, wildly, insanely, rhythmically with the movement of his arm. They sing; he saws off as quickly as he can, as energetically and as fast as he can, first the daughter, then his wife.

Now, turning to us, *you have to punish this man for killing his wife and his daughter in a brutal and cruel manner. The just punishment is to kick this man to death. Kick,* they tell us, *kick this man until he dies. And remember that you will not harbor any more of these foreign-god worshippers.*

And we kick, I kick as hard as I can, quickly, swiftly, we claw and kick, so that the Elder will die quickly, so that he will be delivered to De-us quickly, so he can tell Him that there are many of his believers still waiting, still praying for Him to release us, to give us permission to return to His arms, that we are still waiting. We cannot wait for the world to end, we cannot wait for the faithless to die. And we kick, tear, praying silently, please take the message for us, for prayers have been lost somewhere between the ground and the sky, please take the message, we punch, pull until the Elder is nothing but a heap of tattered flesh, tattered meat, and he whispers, thank you, thank you, and we kick for easy deliverance, for mercy, for forgiveness, and for many things, and he is no more. And our season of betrayal ends finally.

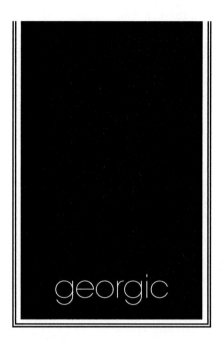

georgic

B odies began to arrive by the dozen, filling the river banks with bodies of men, bloated, like salmon bulging with eggs they must get rid of, their bodies so tightly stuck in the shallows the water could not come or go. So many bodies the color of the underbelly of a fish dead for days. So many bodies ballooned with water, their stomachs not tautly stretched, but filled with water, soft, ready to burst under the slightest of pressure. They have lost the reminiscence of what they must've looked like when they were still alive, working on the land, working on their women, they have become one of many. Anonymous in water they lie face down. They could've been our men; they could've been anyone's fathers or brothers, but we did not recognize them. We went through one body after another, hoping to find the unique scar or mole, or something they carried with them that marked them like no other. But we did not.

No fish dared to pass through this river. The water stilled. Fortified by bodies, the river ceased to be a river and became a shallow waterline lowering and lowering until we discovered more bodies underneath, caught beneath bodies of men.

II

The water leading away into irrigations to feed our fields became the color of the rusty mud, sour-sweet to the tongue, similar to the taste of rusty nails we put in our mouths to make ourselves salivate, the dry saliva forced down our body to lie in the stomach. And even our well has taken on the smell, the taste, turning rusty red, like the color of the un-hungering earth.

Bodies faced the sky, most faced down as if ashamed of the eye in the sky—the sun—that kept vigil over us. These bodies knew shame, hiding their faces from the eye, the vigilant and exacting eye. Birds pecked; stomachs burst with each peck, emitting gas and languid brown liquid, smelling so much like the gums of elders, but stronger, insistent, un-forgiving. The whole village smelled of decay, of aging, of the dead, and we became closer to death with the lack of men, lack of water, and the soiled water we could no longer drink. And when we ate the birds at our most desperate moments, we tried not to think of what they had eaten. We tried not to think of what we were eating. But the birds tasted like no other meat we have ever tasted, sweet and seductive, and like they say, flesh tastes of pomegranate, and once we taste it, once it is impressed into our tongue-memory, meat that comes after never tastes the same. No meat will ever taste that sweet, that complex, as does the human flesh.

Once we had tasted the birds, we knew that the inevitable was next, and we feared the unavoidable, we feared what we would become when hunger became too much.

III

The village has no man except for one boy-man. There are no children under seven years old, as long as the men have been away, our husbands and sons went to follow the call and disappeared from our village. It was not our war; it was not something we understood. Till the land until you can produce enough rice, enough silk, enough calluses on your feet and hands so that your hearts, too, will turn callous, commanded the faceless lord, and we obeyed until our hands chapped, cracked, and hands were covered with brown lines crisscrossing like fates, where the soil had settled between cracks. Give us all able men to fight the war, the lord commanded, and men enthusiastically gathered themselves in the northern corner of the village and waited for someone to gather them; they unfolded themselves from crippling labor and waited to see what lay beyond bodies, beyond the village, beyond the mountains. Our husbands and sons left with a promise of gold that weighed as much as the head of the enemy general or lieutenant, but the promise itself weighed as much as the promise the lord made to gather his soldiers. Later that year, news arrived that the lord and the men from the village all perished in the battle, but no one in the village could confirm the truth because we were bound to the land. No one ventured out to find out whether it was true or not; no one ventured out to see whether the new lord had arrived. For seven years, menless, without labor, we kept tilling the earth, uncropping the land, cropping the land, gathering the greens and husks into our chapped hands. But the land was too big to tend and there were too few of us. We were too powerless to lord over the land. The land suddenly took on a sullen look, as if it were a land we had never seen, and weeds grew alongside the crop, overtaking the crop, overgrowing, until the distinction between what was edible and inedible blurred. No matter how much we ripped the weeds out, they grew fast overnight, greener than the crop, greener than they usually were. We worked faster and faster, ripping out the weeds. We worked with our knees and hands on the ground, surrounded by weeds so high that they almost drowned us. They grew as fast as we ripped them out from the ground, grew more and more strong, taking all the nourishment the land offered until the crops became listless and weak.

IV

And exactly a year ago, exactly a year before the bodies began to arrive downriver to where we were, the sky droned on and on, as if the sky was murmuring to itself. Somebody said that it was the murmur of a god or two, ready to bring down rain. We sighed, knowing that when rain came, the weeds would grow beyond our hands, would go more out of control than they already were. The sun overcast, the sky turned dull beige, then gray. We saw the dark cloud furiously speeding our way; we sighed and unbent our backs, ready to make our way home to be away from the rain, to watch the rain in front of us encouraging the weeds to go higher, higher than they already were. Then the sudden breaking of the cloud, spreading this way and that, until we saw that it was not a dark cloud in the sky, but millions and millions of locusts making their way toward our village. We ran. We ran as the whole sky turned black, turned desperately black as if millions of moons had overtaken the sun, and it was millions and millions of desperate locusts, alive, buzzing, in millions. We ran, shutting the storm windows, shutting out the lo-custs. We fought them, slapped them off of us, slapped them with anything in our hands, and they buzzed, angry indoors, angry to be let out, and we slapped them off of each other, hitting each other with brooms, slapping off the intruders.

The sound droned on and on, then after hours, after hours in the darkness, of whispering, of sighing and knowing what would await us outside, the sound became fainter and fainter until it was only a distant droning.

They carried the news of faraway lands, of the fate of this or that village, many villages in their trail far away and near, of all the labor gone in a few hours, trimmed down to the roots. The locusts carried anguish in their desperate flight, all the memory of anguish both of their own and not their own. And even worse, the dreadful idea of what brought them to our land, what drove them away, what invisible pull made them gather together as one, then leave. We knew, without knowing, what made them so desperate in their search for food. They carried greed with them, and when they left, they left us a barren and finished land, a land so like the autumn land after the harvest, after the bounty of gathered crops, after the human touch, and left us greed, left us a new desperate sense of hunger.

V

And now, after no food, one by one, the villagers found a reason to abandon the land. One by one, after all the wait, after all the failure, they began to leave, saying that hunger made them think the unthinkable, that it was better to live a life of shame, of begging, than having to be hungry for another day. They left with promises of coming back, when the land remembered to give life again, but we knew that their promises were as vain as the promises that the men left with.

And the bodies began to arrive as if they were searching for a home, any home, as if they were searching for mourners, however impersonal, as if they were searching for someone to carry the news back to where they came from.

We could not keep the bodies at bay. We could not keep the men in our village from leaving to fight a war that was not ours. We could not keep the locusts from arriving suddenly one afternoon, ravishing all the harvest. We could not keep the water from dissolving. We have been eyeing the bodies ourselves, we have been looking to them when no one else was, and we, each in each, kept that thought to ourselves, ashamed of a hunger so strong that it made us less human privately, while our words betrayed no thought we had. We licked our cracked lips with our tongues, almost tasting ourselves, then imagining how they'd taste on our tongues.

What remained was the village of women and children and the inevitable, and we could not keep our dark thoughts at bay, or to ourselves.

VI

She lies her way out of the hut. She tells her three children, I have some errands to run. Be good while I'm out, I'll be back before the night comes. Her children nod vacantly, as if they do not quite understand what she is saying, but nod out of habit. The youngest hides behind the two older ones, and she ignores her. And it is a habit, a ritual already between them, an established pattern, a cyclic pattern of shame that comes every time food from the last cycle leaves no traces on the shelf, when the food itself is a long gone memory that the bodies do not remember anymore. She does not realize the cycle: only that she must find food, she must curry favor for all of them to survive.

She stumbles down the mountain already overcast with hints of the day that is about to come. She is part of the mountain, though she has rejected it. She is part of the dawn, though it is not light that draws her forward but hunger and desperation. She knows the way. She has come down the mountain many, many times, enough times to know which crook comes after this one; she knows which can hook her, making her tumble down the steep hill.

She comes down the mountain with shame, bringing a reminder to the whole village that we had failed one of our own, shame small enough that charity has become a dirty idea, something that does not exist in our vocabulary anymore.

To the woman, it is simple; now, she is the only one who can, must, keep her children alive. Has been for seven years: five spent in waiting, and two spent in denying. With the mountain soil too rocky and steep to till, and the land still dense with primitive trees, she cannot open the land, even if she wants, or so she tells herself. She does not know how to hunt—that is her husband's job and her husband has been away for seven years now. She has no relative to move in with, nor does she know anyone—except for one—down in the village, but she knows that she cannot rely on him. She does not owe him anything because she has paid back everything, and in her mind, more.

VIII

She is impractical, and too worn out to beg. The first couple of years after the men left, we took pity on her and gave her what food we could spare, but more and more, we began to accept our state—menless—and perhaps bound to this as long as we lived on this land, and with or without men, we had to pay taxes. Without men, all responsibilities lay heavily on our shoulders, and we could not understand why a woman like ourselves, a woman who was able bodied, could not take care of herself and her family. We did not understand how she could live the way she did, beautiful, but her children covered with lice and grime, who almost never came down to the village. How she held herself distant and apart, not coming down to live in the village, and if she had, we would've accepted her as one of our own, we would've been more merciful. How could she be beautiful in a tragic way, the way dying is blessed and beautiful. And we talked to fill in spaces of hunger, because she was an easy person to talk about: she has the Idiot Son under her strange charm, the Idiot Son has fathered a child, the youngest. Who in this village had children under seven? That's who the Idiot Son learned shrewdness from. We shake our heads in disgust whenever we have to ask the Idiot Son to carry this or that, or do this or that, and he'd undo his robe, take the engorged cock into his hand, and tell us, "Nothing is free. Something for you, something for me. A suck or fuck, I can choose."

IX

She did teach him how to barter, but because nothing comes freely. She did not want to be obliged to him; that's how all of this started. He was the only man—a person— left in the village she could ask for favors, after all the doors remained shut and strangely present to her knocks, as if it were one big body holding its breathe, but pretending to be absent.

The village itself had tightened its lid to the food supply to this woman and her two—or was it three now?—children who lived on the fringes, outside of the village, on their own. They, in our eyes, were neither inside nor outside, but those whose lives were intimately bound to the same fate.

X

She needs food. She must feed her two children; if the husband comes home and finds their children dead, what would he say? But how would she explain about the third child? For seven years, this begging, this continuous begging has been going on, and for seven years, there was not a word or rumor about her husband, or the men from the village. The woman is worn out from begging, but she knows no other way to live. Her hands only intimate with things of the city, she does not know that hands can be used to do anything, if they were taught to be practical. But her hands think like her head, and hands are used to gesture, to help where the words fail.

Now, her hands fail her. Her body fails her. She will fail her two children, and in turn, herself in her husband's eyes.

XI

When she reaches the hut that the Idiot Son lives in, when she knocks on the door once, then twice, a woman's voice, old and cracked, shouts back, "What time do you think it is?"

When the woman tells her that she is looking for the son, the voice inside clucks, then screams that he's already gone to work.

It's an emergency, my youngest is sick, and if she doesn't get better, the other two will get sick, the woman whispers loudly to the door, desperate to call him back, wherever he may have gone to, to call back mercy in the cold distant tone of the mother, to bring back charity. The door suddenly throws open, and there stands an old woman, so old that she peers up from her bent back. Her face deeply etched with disappointments like river crevices during the summer drought, her face darkened with bitterness, that it seems only bitterness kept her going, bitterness the driving force of the will to live.

"Eh, you're that woman who lives up on the mountain, eh?" The old woman squints her eyes.

The woman nods her head vigorously.

"Eh, you're the whore that hunter brought back from the town, and now, you're harassing my son, spreading your mouth and legs open every time you want something from him," her face suddenly changed, eyes squinting until the furrows in her face become deeper, more defined. "You made me and my son into a laughing stock, you've done nothing but cause trouble. Making him steal chickens and clothes and vegetables and rice. You think I'm blind? I don't know? All these neighbors complaining about my son stealing things, about how he goes around half naked, sticking his thing into people's faces every time they ask him to do something. My son wasn't like that until you came down that mountain. After all that we've done for you, you turn around and bring shame to the village."

"Don't," the old woman shouts, closing the door, "ever come near my son, or this house."

XII

Hunger knows no shame, she tells herself as she walks away from the Idiot Son's door. After all that time she had lain on the ground, looking far away from the smell of rotten fish that the Idiot Son on top of her exhaled every time he sighed, she watched the sky move indifferently against the ground, the heaven that never touched the earth like the gods that never seem to care for the pain and hunger that men had to endure, of all the lives that passed, to the heaven and these gods, in a blink of their eyes, as short as the breaths of the Idiot Son moving on top of her. She watched herself on the ground, looking at the sky on her face, unmoved by passion, unmoved by how, at the end of each bartering, he'd touch her cheek with the back of his big, coarse hand, asking her to marry him. And each time, she'd neither push him off nor try to get up, but lay on her back, waiting for the Idiot Son to remove himself from her. He'd keep stroking her cheek over and over, though he never touched any other part of her body; he never ran his hands along the lines of her body. He never pressed his mouth against hers. He never kissed her. He'd keep stroking her cheek until the gentle touch made the skin raw from repetition.

"Marry me," he'd ask, and for a moment, he'd take on the look of a man, any man, not the boy-man he was, his boyish soul caged in the body of a man. "Marry me, and you'll never have to go hungry," he'd say as he kept stroking her cheek, always right hand against her right cheek. She watched the sky moving, and he'd sigh and get what he'd promised: a bag of rice, a dead chicken, eggs, a bolt of fabric. She never asked where they came from. She accepted, like she had done with the Idiot Son's child, without thanks, without a nod because she deserved it, because she had already paid for it.

XIII

She walks down the dirt road toward the center of the village, around the well. Houses are now dark, already beyond the acceptable time for using the fuel. A dog barks as the sky turns gray, air unnaturally thick as if the storm is about to come. The storm does not come. Instead, the moon emerges as big as a house, pulsating and wavering in its bloated state, and it is red, it is blood red. She passes by the river, stinking and foul, and she can't help but to gag. Even in the early darkness, she can hear flies buzzing, still busy on their feasting. And as she gags, as her last remaining humanness makes itself known, she feels something stronger, something so primordial and animalistic that she gags again, not over the smell, but over her own thought. She thinks of making her way home, her way up the lonely mountain, up to the lonely hut where her children await her. She thinks of all this, but her legs will not go forward. She must go, she tells herself, she must not think what she thought, for a minute. But her body somehow has faced the river. She is kneeling on the riverbed. She is touching one of the corpses, bloated. It is dark. There is no one about. It is only the moon, the moon turned blood red, the godless moon we call it here, like the inside of a pomegranate, raw and tender and vulgar, and we, in our houses, as the woman stands by the river, just wait helplessly for the moon to change back, hiding away from the moon as much as we do from our dark thoughts, keeping small like we are meant to do.

The bodies have taken on the color of the moon, like the red lanterns of the city that she had left behind to be with her husband, the light that draws men to the city of whores. The bodies lay still in the shallows, unmoving, unmoved by their death, the woman's hunger. They lie waiting for the distance between bodies and souls to collapse, the distance that can only be closed by the mourners. But she is not their mourner.

She looks around. She reaches over to the closest corpse.

Under her touch, the flesh feels tender, jelly-like, sucking her finger in, and when she pushes hard, the flesh engulfs her finger, then makes an opening, unresisting to her touch. She pinches a piece off with her fingers and closes her eyes. It is darker than the darkness, shutting out all the impossibilities, and only the imagined. Yes, she tells herself, this is not a man, but bean curd, a cake, jelly. Yes, she tells herself, yes, I can eat this, yes, yes. And she does.

And she is the first one. She is not the last. Many will cut their way through the darkness, drawn by the invisible thought, the invisible thread that connects each of us to the river, where the bodies rot; when we think the village asleep, unaware, we will stand by the river, gagging at what brought us to the forbidden riverbank, at the thought of the inevitable. We will close our eyes, all of us, as we taste the first flesh of men. We will swallow. We will close our eyes and feel the jellied flesh sliding down our throats. All of us will do this. And all of us will say, as she said, Yes, yes, I can eat this. Yes, we must, because there is nowhere else, and we must live. This is our land.

fugue

(W)hen I was a child, I was always hungry. We grew up not knowing that some people were never hungry. When I was a child, my parents taught me that our bodies are not ours, but our masters', that we are put on earth to bend as near to the ground as we can, bound in the way seeds are bound to the earth. Our labors were our punishments; our bodies our punishments. We were always hungry, my parents, my brothers and sisters and I. After the harvest, when all we worked for during summer was taken away by our landlord, we ate bark and weeds and things even beasts would not eat. We ate less than three lap dogs that the rich woman in fur always carried around in her arms. The dogs all had jeweled collars, and the fingers of the rich woman in fur glittered in colors we did not think possible, colors we could not have ever imagined if we had not seen her. But now that we had seen her, these colors were the colors we dreamed at night which left our desires unfulfilled. When I was a child, I was always hungry, we grew up not knowing that some people were never hungry.)

(When I was a child, I was always hungry. I grew up knowing that there was a woman who never knew hunger, who always carried three dogs in her arms. She always wore the softest fur, even in autumn when it was not yet cold, and she never walked amongst us. Her small jewel-like shoes made in the city, clean and unused on her, glistened as she sat in her carriage, looking at us. I remember that even her dogs were forbidden to walk on the ground. She was above us, always, she was the woman who never came down to us, and we stayed near to the ground when we saw her, so our worlds never collided. She never talked to us; she never moved. Even our hunger did not touch her. When I was a child, there was a woman who never knew hunger, who always carried three dogs in her arms.)

(When I was a child, there was a rich woman in fur who always carried three dogs in her arms, and when we saw her, we knew that someone never went hungry. She never went to bed knowing what hunger meant. I was only a child, and I only saw her from far away, like all of us, only allowed to gaze at her from a formal distance like beasts behind bars. Then she stopped coming down to the village, and the rumor went that she got sick of living in such a faraway land from where she was from. Then some time after, rumor went that she died. Our Elder told us that the rich people were living in sin, thinking themselves above the land. God is merciful, he lowered his eyes, but God does not forgive sinners. That was the price they had to pay for forgetting about the land, about people's suffering. But she died and we forgot all about her, and we went about our days the same, hungry, toiling the ground, toiling our bodies to live for another day. But this is a story from when I was a child, when there was a rich woman in fur who always carried three dogs in her arms, and when we saw her, we knew that someone never went hungry, never went to bed knowing what hunger meant.)

(When I was a child, there was a rich woman in fur who had three dogs and she taught us that someone went to bed hungry, went to bed knowing what hunger meant, that there are many kinds of hunger and ours was not the worst. She was the child-bride of the man whose dead wife had three dogs. She had to take care of these dogs that she hated, and no one took care of her. She used to go to bed alone, in a big room, in a big bed that could sleep four, no seven of us; I was there, I saw her go to bed by herself, her sighs collecting like husks at the end of the harvest, wind carrying them far, but not far enough, and piling up in a heap by the edge of the field. She would gather her three dogs, but dogs are not faithful; they scampered away and found their own corner to nestle in, and she would cry into her pillow and call them names. She used to make me sleep with her, holding me tight against her like I was a pillow or perhaps her husband who was never home. You can be hungry, my mother used to say, but there are far greater hungers than the one of the body; when your heart is hungry, it can turn you into a ghost, already dead though your blood may run, though you may move like the living, breathe like the living. You are dead when the heart is hungry. She used to cry herself to sleep as she held me tight, and she died soon after in sleep, her arms still around me. When I was a child, there was a rich woman in fur who had three dogs and she taught us that someone went to bed hungry, went to bed knowing what hunger meant, that there are many kinds of hunger and ours was not the worst.)

(When I was a child, I was in love with a woman with three dogs but she never knew me. I loved her, and it was love so real, but I am an old man now, I know that my life is full for having loved her. I was not a child but not old enough to be called a man yet. I was in love with her. She used to come down to our field with her three dogs, and would gaze at the land for a very long time. But I knew that she did not see anything; I knew that she was thinking of something far away. What was her name? I do not remember; it is such a long time ago, and I am a very old man, waiting out my last days in this feeble body. I loved her, though I was merely a boy, and I loved her for all the things people around me weren't: regal, sad, beautiful, and clean. You might ask, is this going to be one of those happy-ending stories, in which she loved me back, and we lived happily ever after? When you are as old as I am, you can tell your children that happy endings are for the privileged few; these are lies we tell ourselves to keep ourselves going in this life, to make this life bearable. No, she was married, had no children, and she died. On the day she was to be buried, I went to her funeral, stood behind everyone, waited until everyone was done with their formal partings, and I touched her cheek, just once, her cheek cold as stone, as cold as the coldest feet, and that day, I became a man, no longer a child, a touch awoke me into a manhood that should've come so long ago. I married another. A good woman. I had many children, many died and some survived. I tried to provide for her because she was a good woman, and in some moments, she became as radiant as the woman with three dogs. And I blamed myself; if I were a better man, my wife would have been as beautiful as the woman with three dogs; my wife's hands would have remained smooth and young. Now, she has died and I miss her more every day. When I was a child, I was in love with a woman with three dogs but she never knew me. I loved her, and it was love so real, but I am an old man now, I know that my life is full for having loved her.)

(When I was a child, I did not know that a happy life, a happy ending is a lifetime where a heart keeps breaking over and over, where we have too many partings. And out of partings comes life itself. When I was a child, I was envious of the woman who came to watch us from her height with three lap dogs in her arms, I was envious of the dogs who never knew how to walk with their jeweled collars. I would close my eyes, lie under the tree and pretend that I was the woman lying on her bed with an arm over my eyes, her bed my carpet of leaves under the tree. I was envious for my parents whose lives were short, who could remain young in my memory, but memory fails me and my love for them, mythical in its heartache. But now that I am older than she ever was, I know that my mother would die of a broken heart if she could see me now. My mother was an old woman before her time. For each birth, she must've lost four teeth that by the time she was done giving birth to the youngest one, she had only one tooth left, but she said that having a tooth makes all the difference. I remember that she never laughed. I don't remember her smiling, only grimacing, her mouth collapsing to one side. My father was the same. He never laughed; he was old like other men in our village and I always thought that people were never meant to look young in our village until I saw the husband of the rich woman. When my father said that they used to play together when they were younger, I looked at him and I looked at the husband, and saw an old man against the middle-aged man. My mother and father were old before their time; by the time I became old enough to remember their faces, they were done aging and they died from a simple cold. They did not grow old enough to see me like this. This is my story and I can make them become young, always young, always happy because I am not. When I was a child, I did not know that a happy life, a happy ending is a lifetime where a heart keeps breaking over and over, where we have too many partings. But this is life.)

love story

I

On the night she died, she promised that she would return, she promised that she would come back to me.

She lay in the middle of the transparent mosquito net, strands of incense smoke trapped within, smoke wavering like thin threads no one could touch. The monk sat by her deathbed, wearing the formal black robe, reading the sutra aloud. Already shrouded in a white robe, the robe for the dead, her robe flowing out, placed formally around her, she looked like a butterfly trapped in a spider's web. A butterfly, a beautiful one, unnaturally earthbound, grounded by the force of the seasonal cycle, neither struggling nor resigned. She looked contained, accepting of the inevitable.

When she saw me, she smiled and struggled to raise herself. The monk paused the death sutra, he stopped the dying process, for a minute, and withdrew himself from the net with a nod, a nod telling me that he could keep death at bay for only so long, a look that said to hurry, for the time was short.

I wanted to go before you came. I don't want you to remember me like this, she said. I don't want you to remember me like this, just give me more time. I'll come back with a better body, a better life, I don't know, a better something. I promise. I don't know how long it'll take me to come back, I don't know, but just wait for me, she said.

She raised herself, and I reached over and touched her face. She pulled away, pulling away the curtain of hair that hung lifelessly around her face; instead, she reached over and she cupped my face with her hands. Already, her hands were cold, as if blood had already left the fingertips to concentrate on pumping the heart.

I'm just tired, too tired, I can't keep this up. I'm sorry, I'm so tired in this body. Please, don't try to stop me, just remember that I'm going to come back to you, she told me.

And before I had a chance to ask her, ask her the most important question, how will I know you, how will I know you with a different face, different body, in a different life? Before I had the chance to ask her the most important question, she closed her eyes, closed herself, and her face collapsed. She breathed in deeply, taking in the smell, inhaling the smell of incense and all that was unfamiliar, foreign to the everyday life, not inhaling me. She breathed in once. And she was dead. The monk reentered the mosquito net and enclosed her face with a white cloth. He warded off her soul as he warded off the trailing smoke with a wave, and lit incense for the dead. He chanted the death sutra, chased off her soul.

I slept in the same room where she was laid out, expecting her to wake up any minute, telling me it's a joke, it's a joke, see, I'm really alive, it's a joke. Her body remained rigid and cold to my touch. I touched her face over and over but she remained formal, already beyond any pain or joy. That she was beyond it all. There was a wake the next night. There was a funeral the following day. Shrouded in white, the color of the dead and the color of the bride, she lay in the coffin. Surrounded by white chrysanthemums, flowers chopped right at their necks, her face was one of flowers, immobile and soft to the touch. We placed a coin on each of her eyes to keep her sealed, for easy passage to the otherworld. Coins to barter her soul entry to the otherworld, to ward off evil spirits. We stuffed cotton in her mouth and her nostrils so her soul would not reenter. We made her as dead as possible and threw the body into the fire.

When the fire died down, we smeared ash all over our bodies, we placed fistfuls of ash into our mouths, and we became one with her.

I mourned for her. I was eighteen years old, but she was my first personal loss, and even until the day I died, she was the only one who somehow wriggled herself to the core of my body as would a worm lodging itself into the core of an apple, eventually collapsing the center, collapsing the skin that shaped the apple, leaving the center coreless and the body formless. I mourn for her, even after all this time. Everything is blurred. I don't know how old I am in any memory, just that something happened, mostly nothing significant. A snippet of vision here and there. But hard as I try, I never remember anything as whole. Like a reflection in water. A sudden movement, and everything wavers, doubles, triples, then disappears.

But I remember this one. When I saw her for the first time, strapped on her mother's back like a rag doll, her neck skewed from no strength in her neck, I told her, I'm going to marry you when you grow up. All the adults laughed, laughing at me, at my sudden aging. At the sudden aging of a little boy who had just recently began to speak. But she looked straight into my eyes and kept looking into my eyes for what seemed like an eternity, then finally nodded. My parents looked at the baby, my parents looked at her parents, and they just nodded. And I knew then, as a three year old, that I would get my wish.

When I turned fourteen, my father decided to send me away. My older brother was going to inherit the land, condemning him to a lifetime of slavery to the poorest of land —better landed than not—making him earthbound to the village, to the family, to the past, though he was the one who should've had a chance to fly away. And I, being the youngest, would get nothing. I would have gladly stayed in the village, I would have gladly spent the rest of my life protecting the land, tilling the land until my body curved into the shape of the planting, but since I was the youngest, since I was the extra mouth, my father could only give me a gift, a trade to carry myself forward into life. He thought of many options – merchant, shoemaker, civil servant, teacher, anything that could condemn me to the life of uprooted wandering. Finally, he decided on studying medicine. You'll always carry your trade with you anywhere you go. You never have to worry about crop failure, drought, poor land, your life will be freer than mine was. This is the only gift I can give you. I was fourteen, and she was eleven. On the day I was to leave, she walked me to the edge of the town. The monk, who was accompanying me—or was it I accompanying him?—told me of the path we would walk, of all the great wonders we would see.

Promise me you will come back, she commanded.

Promise me that you will be here when I come back, I joked.

I'm not going anywhere, I can't go anywhere like you can. This is the only place I'll ever be, I'm stuck here, she said.

Promise me you'll come back to me and take me away, she looked straight into my eyes and commanded.

The monk pretended to look at the sky to read the weather, then he faced the road away, toward the capital that lay somewhere at the end of the road. Without looking at us, the monk urged me that we had to go, we have a long way to go. The monk and I started on our way. I kept looking at my steps, one step at a time, my feet already dirtied from the path, and the only time I did look back, she was still waving her arms as if she were about to take off into the air, as if wishing she could fly.

Throughout the years in the capital, my parents wrote me letters about the news of the village. Who died, who gave birth, which crop failed, which thrived. And always a line or two about her. With each letter, she seemed to get smaller and smaller. I could see her getting thinner and weaker, even with the sparse words they wrote. The last letter I received said that she was no longer seen outside because even with the help of her servants, she could not walk. I had pushed aside these letters, not wanting to believe them. I could not imagine her frail, leaning against this arm or that just to stand. I could not imagine her dying, though I had seen enough deaths in my study as they lay immobile on boards, their insides for all to see and understand. But death, to me, was for others, it belonged to bodies I did not know the names of, I did not know the lives of. And I wanted to keep it far away, not within my arm's length.

She was my first personal death. And she died with a promise.

Soon after her funeral, I completed my study and returned to the village. I watched days pass, hours pass, and everything was the same. As if she never existed. Seasons changed, people died, some gave birth, some left the land. She was disappearing even from her parents' house. No one talked about her. I could not see anything that reminded me of her. Even the face of her mother, whom she took after, began to change, becoming more etched and more distant. She left her mother's face as much as she left without leaving any reminder of her life anywhere. Her parents' grief seemed short. And so did mine. First, I forgot what her voice sounded like. Then her face, one by one, her eyes, the shape of her lips. Soon, I couldn't remember whether she ever existed, though I carried a hollow in my body, where my soul should have been contained. And soon I began to grieve not her, but my forgetfulness.

By the fifth year, my parents urged me to marry. Soon, her parents began urging me to marry.

I promised her I'd wait for her, I always replied, as if that explained everything, but explained nothing at all, even to myself.

She was delirious when she said it. How often have you heard people say strange things when they are dying? You are a doctor, a man of science, you've been at deathbeds many times. How many of them said strange things? my father asked, his kindness somehow wriggling out of his rough sunworn voice.

Yes, people did the strangest things when they were about to leave this world, not thinking about the consequences of their words. How words sometimes shackled the living. How words sometimes chained the lives of the living to those of the dead. They never want to believe that the lives they leave behind go on without them, that lives do not stop when theirs do. The dying are selfish. They don't want to believe that the living are forgetful—though while they were alive, they ruthlessly forgot their dead.

Yes, their words did leave marks, wounding the living. In more ways than one. The young widow whose dead husband cursed her as he was dying, don't you ever think of marrying someone else, you're mine, and if you do, all your children will be deformed. She lived in fear of bearing another child. The first child from the next marriage remained unscathed by the curse. But what about the next one? Or the one after it? She lived in fear, and her new husband hated her more than she ever knew, that bitch, I gave her good money to be my wife, but she's nothing but a stone woman. The new marriage suffered because of the heartless words of the first husband, who, unthinkingly, ghosts upon his wife's life, keeping vigil to the promise long forgotten by the dead. Now, their lives were shackled to a deep silence that cannot be broken.

And her promise. How can I know that she was not like others, binding my life in her death? Even as the village erased the memory of her, even as she began to recede into the past, becoming one of many dead bodies of the village, which kept the village going, the history going forward. Without death, there is no history. But where was this history moving to, to what end? I didn't know. She possessed me with her promise. Her words dragged me toward death, gravitated me toward undoing the mystery of death, opening up body after body, unearthing secret mysteries that people carry in their bodies.

Death makes us, marks us; we carry the dead in us. Beasts are kinder than we are—when they sense their death, they leave quietly, traveling so seamlessly between this and the other world, that we hardly notice their leave-taking. She gave me a hope that could not come true. She made a promise—but was it really a promise? I didn't know. She said that she would return. But the dead cannot return; all the bodies I had pried open, pried apart, searching for the clue

of their histories, clues of what caused their end, these bodies
are proof of their one-way journey to the other world.

Finally, I agreed to marry. I was twenty-five years old.

I was married within a year to a girl my parents had chosen for me. She was pretty, educated beyond the usual, and
she was kind. She was a cultivated girl, the kind who reminded me of a rose. The flower, without human tending, cannot
exist on its own. She carried herself in an artful way, as she
was taught how certain things were done. But I liked her. I
still do. She was what I wanted—pretty, intelligent, kind. I
could think of no one else who would've filled my life the
way she did. I almost loved her, and I did, in my own ways, by
providing for her. She bore me a child, then another, within
five years. I named the girl Love. I named the boy Truth.

But they died.

First, one villager died, a healthy man. One day, he was
healthy and working in his field. A week later, he was dead.
Fever. Sweating. Then discoloration all over his body. Then
his wife died the same way. I began to notice black welts on
their bodies, how their bodies contorted, trying to crawl out
from some small space and failing. But I didn't take notice.
So it began, one villager after another dying. They didn't even
have time to realize that they were dying. By the time fever
overtook their bodies, they were unconscious, spitting out
everything from their bodies. Their bodies protested, tried
to clean themselves from inside out. But not the souls. They
left, not even knowing that they were dying. They left bodies behind, shells contorted so unnaturally that sometimes,
backbones broke, ribs expanded, and the thin skin over their
chest burst. Most of the time, I told the survivors to remain
in the house. They tried to run away, but by the time they
planned their escape, their bodies refused to listen. Fever.

Sweating. Confusion. Contortion. Then her parents. The only thing I could do for them was to massage their backs straight—tying their bodies down to anything straight, unclenching their fists, closing their eyes. For death to look as natural as possible. And I lit the house.

All prayers went unheard. All the medicine, wasted. The monk and I shook our heads, not knowing what to do. One by one, villagers died like grasshoppers in a sudden migration. The monk prayed earnestly, he did. I tended the sick as much as I could, though I knew nothing that would help them. I could only ease their death. When it was time for my parents, when the first signs of the curse appeared, I gave them opium to ease their pain, I gave them extra doses hoping that their transition would be as gentle as possible. Hoping that their bodies did not shame them at the end.

Some miraculously remained untouched. And there was hope in their eyes. They were so close to death, but remained unscathed. I had hoped that my family were the lucky ones, like me, like the monk. That they were the living forgotten by the plague. But they, too, went. When the black welts covered her body, my wife said, Kill me, there's nothing you can do, and asked me to give her opium. She died the way she lived—with dignity, in a formal way. She told me to kill the children to make their suffering less. You brought them into this world, now you are responsible for their lives, whether they are happy, sad; you are responsible for whether they suffer or not, kill them to make their pain go away. I told her that there was no more opium left, and she told me to kill them the best way I could. After she died, I gave them baths as soon as the fever broke their body with sweat. I placed my hands around Love's neck, and pressed her throat with my thumbs. She did not struggle; just accepted as she had done, closed her eyes and nodded. Truth kept calling for his mother, he kept mewling, rolling on his bedding, struggling and clawing at me, clawing to remain in this life. I kept pressing my thumbs against his tiny Adam's apple, pressed it as I apologized, I'm sorry, I'm sorry, as I kept pressing my face against his ear and whispering my apologies; he struggled and struggled, his tiny body resisting me. His mouth open, his eyes open wide; suddenly, he seemed to say, I understand, now, I understand, go ahead, and his arms stopped flapping around. He trusted all his weight to me. I had killed him. I had killed all of them.

Last night, I closed my wife's eyes, washed her body, straightened her limbs as best I could. I wrapped them all in their best robes and closed the door. I left the house, I left all my hopes with the house and set fire to it. It burned. The last thing I remember, I was running toward the fire, the red, burning fire.

II

It was a dare that all started it. Only a dare, nothing but a dare. We did not mean anything by it. It was the same as throwing rocks at sparrows; we throw rocks at them, and they scatter, only to settle back where they were only moments ago, already forgetting those rocks that we did not mean to hurt, but only to show that we were masters over them.

So the dare: we were to meet at four in the morning, when all the lepers came out, when our parents told us never to go out, never to go out, because it was the hour when all the ghosts came out and ate the children alive. When the lepers came out, the bravest amongst us would snatch off a scarf, or a belt, anything they wore and come back with the trophy. It was a simple dare.

There was a house at the end of the village that no one entered or exited. One day, the policemen and some men from the big city came and told us to gather around the house. We all went. It was something new, something different. They told us that this is the house where the lepers lived, and that it was dirty, unclean, that if we entered it, we would all catch leprosy. They told us never to come near this house, and that if we had to, if we touched any one of them by accident, if we drank out of their well or touched their soil, we were to wash our hands and bodies as thoroughly as possible. We all stood around the house and whispered, adults' faces all knowing, as if they had known all along that this house and its residents were different, something to avoid.

But wouldn't it be better if you take all of them away? One of the adults asked loudly.

As of now, only the father's shown symptoms of a leper. Others seem to be okay, but it's in the blood. Any day now, they'll all get it, a man from the big city said, we're taking the father away, no worries.

The house remained quiet, all shutters closed, tightly closed as if to keep the noise out.

And when we all went back to our houses, where it was safe, my mother took me aside, don't you believe a word they say.

I did not believe my mother.

And I did not tell her about my love. I had loved, as a boy does even before he knows the meaning of the word *love*, the daughter who lived in the house of the lepers. She was older, twelve years older. She was my first love. I knew when I first met her in her house before it was boarded up, before the light was exiled from the space, that she was the one, the one I was to love for the rest of my life. That was before the disease shut her up along with her family, though she must not have had the disease, even that night when the dare game turned into something malicious, even after she was taken away to an island far off that no one knew the name of. But

I knew then, if I could not love her, then I would spend the rest of my life alone, always missing a part of myself, a part of my soul. And when we were alone for the first time, when she sat by the window, looking out, her white neck strained to see the outside, I touched her neck gently as I have seen in the movies my mother took me to once in a while without telling my father, the movies of white men and women gently touching each other as if each was a porcelain doll, ready to break at the slightest of pressure. She was startled, looked suddenly at me as if I were a man, like the way those white actresses looked at the men.

Don't grow any older.

She laughed. We all grow older.

I don't want you to grow older. Wait for me to grow older. Wait till I can marry you.

She laughed like a bell and gently touched my face. I can't marry you. I'm too old.

I don't want you to get older.

She reached out, stroked my cheek again, slowly, and even when her hand left my cheek, I felt a phantom hand still on my cheek. I can't, and there's a reason, even if I weren't older. Besides, when you get older, you'll fall in love with a girl of your age, and you'll never remember that you made this promise.

I know what I know, and when I get older, I'm going to marry you, I'm going to protect you...

She smiled sadly, and the way the light entered the room, only her mouth was lit. I can never marry anyone, ever.

And it began as a dare. We sneaked out of the house between the hours of tiger and rabbit, and met by the abandoned shrine. We knew that that's where they all gathered. I now know that that's where they gathered to pray to make themselves human, not sick, not limbless, not shadowed and buried in their houses, but as a boy, I only knew that that hour when the night and the day almost met, but not quite, was the time when they appeared. As we hid in the bush, we strained our eyes in the darkness, letting our eyes seek out movements in the dark. And they appeared. Here, a woman that we thought had died five years ago; the girl, her head wrapped in a scarf, the girl, my love. A man without a leg, holding onto a woman. They all began to gather, otherworldly like ghosts, silent, not talking to each other. They sat here and there, all like stone statues, not moving, not talking, just quietly, as if they were all talking to their private god each in each.

And a battle cry. We shot out from our hiding places, each with rocks and sticks in our hands, and ran out. They stood up startled, then froze. We began to throw rocks at them, and with each thud, we knew we hit our marks. When all the rocks were gone, we began to hit them with our sticks. I threw rocks at my girl because all the kids were throwing rocks at her. We hit the man without his leg, and he hopped away crying, and we chased him around the ground, down the steps, then up the steps again, and finally back to where we started. He hopped slowly, and when we caught him, we made sure not to touch him but hit him with our sticks. One of us snatched away his crutch, and he cried and cried, and he was one of the men I knew, but we kept hitting him and throwing anything at him—bottles, rocks, marbles. It was a game. A cruel game, but a game, because we've heard about lepers, we heard about how they were forgotten by the gods, how the gods hated them so that's why they got leprosy. We left the man whimpering, and turned to the only person left: the girl who hadn't moved, while others had ran away, dissolving into the darkness. We snatched her scarf, an older boy ripped off her clothes, we kept hitting her with sticks, though she was my love, because she was my life, and I started to cry as I hit her, lightly, pretending to hit her, because everyone else was hitting her. Because everyone else was having fun hitting her, and I couldn't betray myself. I cried quietly, hitting her lightly where it hurt the least, on her legs, until one of the older boys said that he was going to rape her, and he unbelted his pants. We stopped what we were doing mid-movement; we held our breath. All was still, even the girl, as the boy moved on top of her roughly, his breath becoming louder and louder and until he screamed out and she just lay on the ground, her body glowing blue, her eyes closed like she was already dead, like she was already dying. And when the boy ended his jerks with a cry, cracked with his voice breaking, when he turned to us and told us that we can't tell what happened to anyone, ever, or he'll cut off our penises, telling us that it's time to go home, we stood there. With our eyes, we told each other, without the boy seeing, we didn't see anything. We didn't see anything. It was our pact.

The girl lay there naked, unmoving, as if she were dead, and we made our way back home.

We laughed and joked uneasily the whole way until we saw our houses slowly emerging in the dawn, and we hushed ourselves. We quietly, all too quickly, said goodbye with a slight nod, each of us disappearing into our windows. And I reached my house. Under all the laughs, I hated myself for not being big enough to push the older boy aside, I hated myself because I was small and powerless, and as soon as I quietly made myself lie down, I cried into my pillow.

And I still see her as she was that night. When I think of her, even after all these years, my heart breaks at the memory of her, so white and small in the darkness, naked, not moving, as if she had submitted herself to the darkness all around her and what had happened to her, as if everything was, for her, already something impersonal, a life that was borrowed for a lifetime. I see her suspended in the darkness like a small star in the sky, darkness all around her, cold and small. I do not know who took her scarf, nor who took away the man's crutch as their prized possession.

For a long while, we boys forgot about the night, the night of the great attack. We forgot, dared to forget, because we had seen the unspeakable. Whenever the younger boys saw the older boy, we all tried to pretend he was still our leader, though we knew that his reign would be done, as soon as he was old enough to be sent off as an apprentice in some trade in a faraway town or city, far enough away to stop our reminders. We silently watched for any sign of punishment on his face or hands, but his face only broke out in acne and his hands were as smooth as they had been, a pair of hands that knew no pain or labor. And when he went away several years later, we were older by then, and we had forgotten about what had happened that night. I didn't, but it did not matter whether I had forgotten or not as long as I did not show that I had remembered. She had become more withdrawn into herself, she was diminishing more and more like the memory of the night in my mind, dissolving into the dark.

But the policemen from the city had not forgotten about the lepers. They came in their blues and blacks, imposing their authority with their flashy sticks and medals, they came once a season, then more frequently, until my mother whispered into my ears, quietly, as she pulled the cover tighter around me one night, They may take the family away. I pretended to sleep, kept my eyes closed and didn't move. As soon as she got up and left my side and shut the door, I held my breath, and waited for the house to quiet down. My mother was restless. She kept shuffling her feet, pacing, sighing, and I could hear her sighs where I was. I kept quiet until I heard no more sighs, no more sound, and got up. I knew what I had to do, I had to see the girl before they took her away. Before she was beyond my reach or before she disappeared like her father. Before no one talked about her anymore. I packed my schoolbag with a change of cloths and all the money I had kept in the bottle and quietly left the house.

I ran and ran in the dark, I knew where I had to go. I knew where she lived. I ran as fast as I could, I knew that if I missed this chance, I would not be able to tell her, ever again.

When I reached their house, a small shack on the outskirts of the village, windows boarded up, like that night, I picked a rock from the ground and threw it against one of the boards. The stone made a loud clutter sound, then rolled off onto the ground, beyond my reach. The house remained quiet, as if there were someone inside, but holding their breath. I threw another rock. Another moment of silence, then whispers, like several voices talking as if consulting, in a hushed tone.

A woman's voice—young, still smooth and melodious—whispered, Who is it?

It's me, I whispered back.

A pause, as if they were trying to figure out who it was, as if they were collectively asking each other who it was without uttering.

The board slid open an inch; a white beautiful hand thrust itself out to push the board wider so that they could look out, but not for me to look in. But I knew; the hand had the same glow that the body had that night, bluish from impoverishment of light, the hand that glowed, like a beautiful gem, like a moonstone. I knew the hand belonged to the girl. I grabbed it with both of my hands; the hand flinched momentarily, jerking once at the sudden touch, then relaxed, but remained hard and lifeless and cold in my hands.

They're going to take you away, I whispered urgently, you have to run away before they do.

I know, the voice replied, but I'm not going anywhere.

Why? They'll just shut you up on some island and you'll never get away. Let's run away together. I have some money, let's run away.

I'm tired of being shut up. I don't mind going...

You can't go without me. I'm going with you... I promised you.

Oh, are you that same boy? You've grown. You are so much taller now.

I gripped her hand tighter. You have to run away. They can't shut you up.

I'm already shut up. What's the difference—being shut up in my own house or being shut up on an island... At least we can go outside and feel the sun on that island.

She withdrew her hand slowly, Thank you, but I'm tired of being shut in darkness.

Grabbing her hand harder, I begged her to go away with me, but her hand became more and more hard, more unresponsive. I knew that her mind was already made up; she wanted to leave. She wanted to not think of this village that had abandoned her and her family, that had made her life, for the past ten years in their house, like a death already forgotten. I understood, even as young as I was, that she was tired. That she missed the sun. That she missed not being alive.

I knew. My hands relaxed themselves without prompting.

Her hand lingered on the edge of the window sill.

I reached out and touched it gently, stroked it like the way she had stroked my cheek so many years ago, like the way I had stroked her white neck so many years ago. I'm sorry about that night, I whispered, then turned and ran back to my house, crying all the way home.

That was the last I saw of her or talked to her. The next night, my mother came to my side and whispered, they have taken away the family. That was the last I heard of what happened to them, and I never loved anyone for the rest of my life.

III

My mother warns us not to talk about it. She says that there's nothing to talk about. We are who we are, unable to drain out the curse that runs in our blood, unable to choose who we are, or who we are to become. My mother warns me never to tell anyone about where we're from, no matter where we go, who we are. It has no name, we cannot reveal ourselves to anyone, especially them. Everyone knows about *it*. *It* lives in the house built outside the invisible village boundary. *It* is the line on our registries that cannot be erased, no matter who we marry, no matter how many times we change our names, faces, residences like cocoons shedding their casing in order to become a new possibility. There is no possibility for us, my mother tells me. It is what makes us dirty like pigs; it is what makes us work with dead bodies, washing them, cleaning them, touching them in places where they themselves never touched.

And we are *it*. And my mother tells me that she has a cousin and that he's coming to live with us, because we're *it*, and he is one of us, and now that he has broken the rule, he can never live among *them*. She tells me never to tell anyone about this cousin, I can never tell anyone about him, she says.

And when he comes, he is as thin as the willow tree outside my window, carried in by my father like he is a log for the fire on a long winter night that we keep lit to warm bodies, above the freezing temperature. Except that now it is late summer and we don't need this fire until the end of October. When he comes, he carries with himself an old, small bag that he can cover and hide with his two big bony hands, apologizing that everything he owns is contained in it—some papers, some clothes, and mostly the past we do not know. When my mother opens her arms to him, he mimics her gesture, and he, too, opens his arms slowly like an embarrassed heron—he later tells me that herons are the only birds that can get embarrassed—and falls into my mother's arms and bursts out crying. Suddenly as he starts to cry, his sobs stop in midnote, and he looks around as if suddenly awakening from a troubled sleep, only to tell us he is tired and he must sleep.

And he sleeps for days, weeks, he sleeps for a hundred years like a stone that knows nothing else but to sleep. He does not move. He doesn't make any sounds. His eyelids are as big as the coins my father has to place on dead people's eyes when villagers bring them in to be cleansed because it is his job to take care of the dead, because no one can touch the dead body except for *it*—us—and because somebody has to place coins on their eyes so that the dead can pay their way to the other world.

I watch him sleep. His eyelashes move in the rhythm of his sleep, and I touch them with my fingertips, like I am touching a moth, gently so that it does not tatter under the touch. He twitches; I flinch. And I run as fast as I can back to my father's workshop where a body lies waiting to prepare itself for the short journey to the grave. As I help my father lift the rigid and heavy legs up so that he can pull clean underwear over the body's hardened buttocks, I think of my cousin, soft, breathing, back in the room. He is the only one who seems alive and present in this house of the dead, this house for the dead. As we adorn the body, one by one, with its departure clothes, clothes so fine that I think how shameful it is that it will all be buried when it is set into the ground, I think of him. How he sleeps so indifferently. So gently, his face still and mask-like, of his long and delicate eyelashes. And next time I go back into the room, I gently place a cloth over his face, and when it moves with his breath, I am relieved that he is still alive, still here, and I breath in sync with him.

When he awakens, he walks around the house without a sound. He doesn't talk very much, and when I ask him about his home, about him, he looks out the window like he's looking for wherever he came from in the field across from us. He finally says that if he hadn't been *it*, it would've never happened. And I wait for more, like a hungry chick with its mouth open, waiting for more of him, more about him, hungry for him. After he looks more into the field, he says that he thinks of the things he did, and he thinks that he never did it, like he had dreamt it in his long sleep. He rubs his left hand over his right arm and gently tugs at his cuff, then touches it. My mother sits by the table and folds clothes to put over bodies, and tells him that now that he's here, far away from where he has been, everything is different and that he can start his life over. He looks at her and cries without making any sound. My mother talks of this or that, changing the subject as rapidly as mosquitoes that flicker in and out of our sight in the summer night. He looks at my mother talking, and he is somewhere else. Like he is looking at what's inside my mother, something that isn't beneath the flesh, as if he's searching for a ghost or a past in my mother's face.

It's been five years now since he came. I have watched him day in, day out, even while he sleeps. He helps my father, and he is better with the dead than he is with the living. When

I watch from the dark corner late at night as he works on a body, I listen to him cooing lullabies to them to gentle their last sleep. He gently places clothes here and there, hides their private parts with clothes so that they will not be ashamed to know that they were exposed under the touch of a stranger, under the gaze of *it*, and all the while treating them with the dignity that they would never have offered us while they were alive. My cousin quietly watches all the transactions between my father and the villagers from the Departure Room, as I now watch him befriending the dead from my shadow.

He does not know that I have watched him. He is a mystery after all these years of sleeping in the same room, eating in the same room. He betrays nothing of himself, nothing of *itness*, nothing of his past. And once in a while, between the coos and gentle touches, he rubs his wrists hidden under the long-sleeved-shirt cuffs that he wears even during the hottest summer, as if there is a phantom ache. That is the only time he becomes someone less mysterious and more human, someone with a past hidden in his gesture.

Late at night, in the dim light, my cousin talks to the dead. He hears something I cannot hear, no matter how much I strain my ear while I fold them into their departure clothes, no matter how many bodies I have addressed. Late at night, I see him nodding and responding as he stuffs cotton in orifices, moving his mouth with the rhythm of the cotton entering, lodging into unwilling flesh. I hear the gentle incomprehensible words coming out of his mouth, sounds forced out as if he has pebbles in his mouth and every word sounds so deep and hard and he can never chew or swallow them, so he spits them out one by one, carefully. And late at night, when I am not in the workshop with him, I repeat the sounds I heard into my pillow, imitating his sounds until I get it right, so that one day, when he speaks his secret language of the dead to me, I can talk to him.

As much as he is quiet, the bag he brought with him still contains a bigger mystery. More and more bodies begin to arrive with the war that's started, and we become the transit point for bodies between the warfront and their homes, to make our brave soldiers more presentable so that they do not shame themselves in the end. We keep our hands busy, and we feel more needed, more important, among the empire of the dead. He has become more a part of the family and less a stranger. His bag still contains mysteries, still contains stilled past and so does his gesture. I have spied on him, I have watched him, and now, he has begun to watch me, too, but I have never dared to open his past. Sometimes, I have seen him standing over a body, sewing up an orphaned arm to an armless body, and suddenly, he stops in mid-thread, wipes his hands against his apron, and takes out a photo from his pocket. With the tips of his fingers, he looks at it, stares at it, forgetting to breathe, and I forget to breathe with him. Moments pass after so many missed breathing cycles, and, exhaling loudly, he puts it back into the pocket of the apron. The photo must contain a key to his past. And I want so much to see it, to see him in that photograph, to find him. I am hungry for him.

My father tells our cousin that now that he is a part of the family, he must think of settling down. Now that I am older, now that I am of the age, it is better that we marry. Besides, my father lowers his voice as if he is afraid of his voice being carried by the night toward houses in the village, he tells us that we can never marry one of them; besides, and my father averts his eyes, looks down, you know what happens when we try to get above ourselves by wanting one of them. Yes, my cousin says, yes, he knows.

No one comes to our wedding. No one is invited. No one officiates. We quietly go to the city hall and sign a new registry: I, the daughter of *it*, and he, the son of *it*. My mother adorns me in brown clothes that symbolize that we are not purely white, a color easily dyed into any color, easily moldable in any situation, but that our color is already decided, and no color mixes well with brown. And that night, my parents go into the Departure Room to sleep with the dead while we are left in our usual room by ourselves, with one bed and two pillows.

My cousin—my husband—and I sit across from each other, facing each other, and the first thing I tell him is that I want to see the photograph. He looks up, startled, and looks down. Why do you want to see the photo, he asks, and I tell him because I have watched him ever since I was small, I have watched him stare at the photo. I want to know him, I tell him, I want to understand.

He sighs. Then he tells me to wait, and when he comes back, he has the photo in his hand. He gently touches it with his fingertips, stares into it longingly as if he knows that it may be the last time he can ever look at it, and as if he must memorize it. Then, without looking at me, he hands me the photo curled around the edges, a photo, faded from years of exposure and touch, of a barely visible face of a woman.

He tells me that he had loved her, but she was one of them. That when she found out that he was *it*, she married another.

He tells me simply, and I understand. I understand now of the distance he has kept with them, I understand the hollow look he has been carrying for the past five years, and I understand myself more through his pain, of how, many days, I have stood in the bathroom, scrubbing my skin over and over and over until my skin turned raw and red and painful to the touch, sometimes blood trickling out from too much scrubbing. How I still did not feel clean because no one touched what I touched, telling me that I am *it*. Like how I would go over to friends' houses, and the mothers would tell me that they could not let me in. They cross the path when they see us coming. They throw salt over places where we had been to ward off curses. They keep their distance. Only when somebody dies and their grief becomes overshadowed by the practicality of having to clean the dead do they come to our house at the outskirts of the village, telling us of the job to be done. All these accumulated images slide into the silence, and after all these years, with his words, I understand what it really means to be *it*. That there is an exacting distance between them and us; that we can never try to shorten the distance.

I touch his cheek gently to let him know I understand. I keep touching his stilled face, over and over, until his face collapses, crumbles, and he sobs into my hand. He cries that he does not understand why he was born if he is to live the life of a beast, why he must endure this shame, this treatment. How his life seemed to have ended the day she got married. I am ashamed, he says, I am nothing. I press my lips against his cheek, I press my lips down his neck, down the hollow of his collar bone, down his arms as I tug his shirt open, then down, and when I kiss his elbow, he cries out hoarsely, don't look, don't look. But I keep pressing my lips. I open my mouth to tongue the red scars as he cries, don't look, don't. I tongue them, one by one at the slash marks, red and thick moving quickly in beats. I tongue them one by one, slowly like an animal licking away the wound. I lick them one by one, murmuring, it's okay, it's all right, I know what this is, I can't make them go away, we can try to, but I can't make your scars go away. These are scars for each week she betrayed you, each week that she did not meet your gaze or answer your letter and the rumors and the marriage; I cannot make them go away as much as I cannot change it, as much as we are bound in the servitude of the dead until we, too, become one of them; we cannot drain cursed blood from our body by slashing our wrists and elbows. All the tension in his arm melts under my tongue; he says they never go away.

I tell him I cannot take them away, yes, they will never go away, but I am here now.

song

Once upon a time, when the world was still young and impressionable, when gods lived amongst men, and men amongst animals, there was no death, no sickness. No one died and no one suffered. Pain was still a word that did not exist. Once upon a time, before the world was divided up by borders and names, the land was one, an island surrounded by sea. Everything men wanted, they had, and no one wanted anything because all that they ever needed was given to them just by thinking. They imagined, and they got. There were no words like envy or jealousy, the words in this world were few, but enough.

Before our village burned, before the Enemy pushed the border and broke into our land, we did not know of anything except seasonal changes. Our enemy then was the sun, the rain, air. Our enemies were something bigger than us and we did not fight them but just accepted them. When there was too much sun, the earth cracked open; when there was too much rain, the water flooded the land, washing away our crops. We were simple and blamed gods when our land failed us, when we failed our land. We were hungry; we were full. We thirsted until our lips cracked and lost their red; our throats were lubricated with the coldest of water during summer. But our land was ours. It was no one else's.

There was no north, no south, no east or west. There were no boundaries that marked us from others; what was ours, was theirs, and what was theirs was ours. There was no sun that grieved us nor rain that brought forth suffering. All was just and all was within reason, within gods, who were simple and just like children, because we were all children, after all.

Then the Enemy came. We had been warned by the voices that floated out of the radio, but we did not believe them. We thought that everything they said was made up, created by some men far away who joked at our expense, our isolation. They said that people were hungry in cities everywhere, they told of how many men died that day honorably for the war, but we did not feel the wind of war touching us, we did not see anyone from the cities begging us for food. We carried ourselves the way we had done for many years, imitating the ways of our mothers and fathers, who imitated their own mothers and fathers, and the way we lived was with the land, with the rhythmic cycle of the land. We did not believe them. Not the voices.

Then one day, a man stood by the sea and wondered what was beyond the sea. A Hog told him that there was nothing beyond the sea, that the water just circled around and would take him to the shore on the other side of the island, but the journey through the water was perilous and long, that there was nothing, no living creature, no man. This Hog was a teller of tall tales. He exaggerated his importance, they all knew, and the man doubted the words that came out of the Hog. But the man wanted to see. He built himself a boat and headed out onto the sea to see, despite the pleas from his people, from his gods, from his animals.

When the Enemy came, we feared that the earth was breaking open with their rolling machines the size of a house, machines that carried men inside their wombs like babies, but these were not babies. They were men that looked like us, and when the mayor came out of his hiding place (we all held our breath, we held our breath and watched him) with a white cloth (we laughed quietly, a shirt? Or his underpants?), walking toward the machines with one hand holding a stick with the white flag and the other holding up the sky, the men looked at him, raised their guns and shot him down, the first shot making him topple over with a questioning look, then he became a beehive with red blood pouring out. All the machines opened at the top, spat out men like women giving birth all at the same time, twins, triplets, and they dragged us out, one by one, from under beds and tables, kicking open the doors.

This man rowed the first day, but he soon became tired so he rested his arms. He looked up at the sky, and the gods wailed at him, how can you leave us, how dare you leave us, don't you know that you can't live without us, as much as we can't live without you? They wailed and rocked his boat here, there, raising a storm around his boat, rocking his boat so that he would submit to their pleas, but he did not. He ignored them, held on tight to his small boat; the waves, with the encouragement of the gods, gripped his body, but he held on. They caused waves to swallow him, but he held on. The gods wailed and felt betrayed, and the storm raged on, with a man on his boat not submitting to the gods.

They dragged us one by one, pulling our hair or our collars, holding under their arms those that were small, if they were struggling. My husband told me to not get out, to hide in this barrel, hurry, he will put the lid down, do not come out until he tells me, hurry, hurry, and he lifted me up, my stomach getting in my way. I can't sit here, my stomach's too big, I whispered back to him. You have to make yourself fit, fold your legs under you, hurry, we have no time, I promise I'll come get you, but they're searching houses now, and he pushed me in. I held my breath against the stink of the barrel. He shut the barrel, then rolled it on its side to make it seem like it had always been there, with other barrels, on their sides. The banging of doors, screams, then shots. Shots, screams. I held my mouth to keep from screaming, from screaming with others; in the dark, I could not see, and my stomach painfully pushed against the sides. The dark only created images of shouts, of screams, all the cattle-screams we had heard during the cleaving days. And I prayed.

The man's throat contracted in want of water. He did not know that his throat contracted in rhythm with the sea, the waves around him. His saliva, the thick liquid that had come naturally to him on land, had dried up. The sea was still, too still. The oars had been swallowed up during the night of wrestling with his gods. They now rested on the bottom of the ocean, now separated from their twin half, the first man made objects to be mocked, without defenders. The man lay on his back and let the boat carry him back and forth in the same place like the cradle of a child rocked by an invisible hand. The sun was unforgiving. It glared at him, never for once blinking, and he lay on his back with his mouth open, then closing, his tongue tasting the salt on his lips, he tasted the ocean on his lips.

The darkness made time elastic; it stretched, then contracted, and I waited for my husband to tap on the barrel to tell me that it was safe to come out, it is safe, the Enemy has gone. But he did not. I waited in the darkness, my legs already divorced from my body, my arms no longer felt like mine, something that did not belong to me. Screams died down; the bullets died down. The earth shook as the thunderous machines rolled away, the thunder receding farther and farther until it was only a slight tremor of the earth, then nothing. The earth quieted down; the storm had passed. I pushed the lid away with my head, but it did not budge. I kept pushing and pushing, but my husband's fear was stronger than my desire to breath, my desire to stretch out my limbs, to reclaim them as my own. His fear kept the lid on, held tied, and for a moment, I feared that I would die in the barrel from starvation, from my blood freezing in unmoving limbs, and they would find me, weeks and weeks from now, in a barrel, and they would laugh and cry about how they had forgotten me. My child inside of me kicked me, telling me that she must live, I must live, I must open the lid before I kill her.

He closed his eyes. The night had come. The sea was, like during the day, still, only a slow rocking that lured him to sleep. He closed his eyes and let himself fall into a gentle dream, but what waited in the dream was not gentle. It was a wailing god who appeared in his dream, a god, a child, who asked him why he was abandoning her, why he was not happy. The man blinked in his dream eyes, then found himself in the village where he was born, where his people were, asking him in a chorus, why was he curious about other lands, why was he questioning the way they lived, why why why.

The man tried to speak; he tried to explain that a beast had told him that there was nothing in the sea, but he wanted to see, to experience it himself. He wanted to experience a place where there was nothing, no living creature, no man. It was only the second night of his journey, but he had experienced nothing except that beyond gods, beyond the land, there was really a mysterious world where things were still, where things did not move according to his will. The Hog was right. But the gods had taken away his voice; his tongue felt like a stone in his dry mouth, even in his dream mouth.

When I finally burst open the lid, staggering for want of space, the village was quiet as if the early night had fallen to keep the dead at bay, but it was not yet the Day of the Dead, it was not yet night. I stepped out of my door; the door creaked open, amplified more because of the still-life painting in front of me. Even beasts had lost their voices. Men and women and children all lay on the ground, some on their backs, some on their sides, some on their faces, these bodies all made imperfect with holes. Any minute now, I told myself as I held my stomach, they would all get up, laugh, and tell me it's a joke, only a joke, a joke set up by the voices on the radio, a joke. No one moved. Their faces anonymous in the way beasts' faces were, individuality erased in the way days could be shaved from worries. Only when I looked closer did these faces make sense. There, my next door neighbor. There, a man with a cross on his chest, our priest. Here, by my feet, was a child who lived in the house next to the priest's, who used to steal apples from our yard. My aunt lay on her back with her skirt hiked up to her stomach, with her legs wide open and her mouth wide open; a child lay near her in the shape of a throw. Everywhere, men and women and children lay in the postures of their last moments. I screamed, but nothing came out; my throat contracted, bottling up all the screams and fear, and the child inside of me kicked as if screaming for me because I had lost my voice.

The man woke up from his dream. He was not in his village, but where he left himself, in the boat, in the sea, aimlessly wandering the sea. He was the first wanderer, to wander from his village, from his gods. He tried to conjure up water, but the gods had made a pact amongst themselves. They had erased the gift of granting what he desired. No more, they said amongst themselves; in the village, the topography of desire was real, water was here, food was there, and all they had to do was to walk to the place of desire. Here, in the sea, his desires were erased because he became curious and abandoned them. He was their enemy; they taught a new word to the people on land; those who did not follow their way of living was the enemy. He became the enemy of the men, of gods, of beasts. You must guard your land from the enemy, they taught men, for the enemy will disrupt your ways, will take whatever, change, yes, change your way of life.

My husband lay on the muddy street like a rotten apple that had fallen onto the ground and been stomped, bruised, his outline distorted from the blows, his head indented and crushed. His beautiful face half gone, with his arm stretched out to the body of a woman near him, her hand also stretched out to him. She lay on her back with her face toward him, her neck strained, then frozen in the posture of death, her thighs wide open in a way that no woman's legs could be open, her breasts taut even in death. But it was not just a woman; she was his mother. Suddenly, someone tugged my skirt, and I tried to scream. A joke, a joke, I wanted that person to say with fake painted blood on his face, but it was a girl, a girl who was not yet a woman, a girl that had lived in the house near ours. Everyone's dead, she said, my mother's dead, my father's dead, my little brother's dead, everyone's dead. She slipped her hand into mine; everyone's dead, she kept repeating herself. A cow moaned, mourning for the pain in her udder, perhaps also for the hands that soothed the ache, in the precise cycle of the sun.

He had been in the sea for many days, and he saw only gods taunting him with waves that did not move, the sun that kept vigil over his slow wasting, and at night, stars and the moon that took over the vigil from the sun. He knew that he must be dying; he did not know of anyone who died in the village, for gods had kept death at bay, and it had not entered the vocabulary of men yet. He would be the first one in the short history of men to die, he told himself, though he himself did not know what it felt like to die, nor what death meant. Maybe it was like the trees shedding their leaves in autumn, or perhaps like the sun that must go down every day, only touching the night briefly, in the moment when the orange of the horizon mixes with the dark blue of the night, creating purple, the ray of purple.

To the east is the border, to the west, our village, and we must go east now that our homes are gone, the girl said to me. There was no one alive; everyone lay on the ground, carelessly placed, all clutching the earth to protect the land, or perhaps they did not die to protect us. They died because the Enemy came, because they were pushing the border eastward, and ours was the one, perhaps the first one, to be trampled down to the ground, our people first to fall. The girl said that we must go now, before they come back, we must go east to seek help, that's what her parents said before they died, to go east. Where the sun rises from. And we walked, we have walked like this for many days now. We have been walking toward the sun when it came over the mountains, then against it, with our backs turned, as it moved across the sky in an arc, back toward where we came from. As the sun set, we prayed that this is all a dream, our village still intact, our houses containing all that we left behind, our past, our future, and our people. But the girl knew; she said that the Enemy is like that, there is no mercy. It kills, it violates, it runs over whatever gets in the way. I silenced her, and she walked like an orphan. She is an orphan, as much as I am, orphaned from our land, our people, and we only have each other to take our stories with us.

The gods did not pity the Enemy. People he had grown up with, his people, did not pity him. He was the Enemy. He has broken away from us, the gods told the soothsayers and in dreams of men, he has rejected us, now he is an orphan, an exile. He has betrayed us, his own people, his own land, people in his village whispered amongst themselves, and the birds carried the whispers back to the gods, and the gods smiled. He has abandoned it all, the gods whispered in dreams, and the price of betrayal is death. Our Enemy, who built a boat out of curiosity to see a better world, a larger world, a dream that the world was bigger than we gave. There is no mercy for the one that breaks the rule, they told the people.

We have gone through the landscape filled with bodies, all mutilated, all imperfect from wounds the Enemy caused; we have gone through villages with no houses left, burned down to the ground, leaving blackened squares and rectangles on earth. We have gone through fields of what used to be pastures, now homes of freshly made mounds. To the east is the border, to the west, our past. Nightly, the eastern horizon is lit up in bonfires of a war we do not know the name of; it is the role of the historians in faraway cities to name the war. They will give a name to the Enemy. Let them make us into numbers, let them fret their nights asking the why's. Here, we are walking east to the border, though that's where our Enemy is. We crawl on our knees and hands to lap up water from the ground. We have caught ants and worms and stuffed them in our mouths. To the east lies the future, to the west, the erased past. We walk through battlefields and men begging to be killed, of men crawling on their missing limbs, falling over; of once-domesticated dogs and cats feasting on their masters and the crows pecking on men still alive, too weak to shoo away the dark birds. Flies buzz so densely that we keep our eyes shielded and our mouths shut so that they will not lay eggs on the vulnerable parts of our bodies. We walk through the nightmare landscape where the living are dead, and the dead walk amongst the fallen to pick goods to carry back where they came from.

As he looked up to the sky one night, his limbs powerless and heavy and his throat cut apart by thirst, a child-god appeared in front of him, sitting near him with a look of awe. He thought of how soft she looked, how she would be easy to strangle, to tear away her limbs and eat, and the child-god smirked, then smiled. I'm not supposed to be here, you know, she said, but I wanted to ask you why you were not satisfied. None of my family knows that I am here; why did you want to see other things, what was so important about seeing other worlds that you would exchange your soul for it? Why are you doing this to yourself when all you ever needed, we gave you freely. He closed his eyes to ward off the child-god, but she followed him to the dreamland. Why? He blinked, pushed her voice away, willed her gone, but she followed him into the next dream, what else did you need? We gave you everything, but what made you want to see other worlds? She threw questions at him like a child, and she was a child. He asked her what dying meant. She held her breath suddenly, intake so sharp that it rang in his ears. Then softening her voice, she asked him how it felt to die, how it feels now, knowing that he might die. He asked her, where do we go when our bodies disappear? She paused. I don't know, you're the first death we've ever had. We never dreamt that someone might die. But you have volunteered to be the first—we will see. He nodded in his dream body, and she stayed with him.

The past weighs heavily on our backs, in our hands, though we do not carry anything. It is memory we must carry with us as we take one step at a time toward our future. We did not know how much the past weighed until we carried it on our backs, when we hoisted up the stories of our past onto our backs. With each step, we discard this and that detail, prioritizing what is important, and we become lighter and lighter, but wearier. We discard what is really needed to keep our story short. Details have no meaning; details are not essential for our survival. The east, the east, that's what we know, to the east is the future. But we do not know where the east begins, whether we have entered the land of the east, for there is no demarcation that separates the east from the west, our past from the future. It is all like the land around us; we pass village after village as if we are reliving that day, as if we are passing our village over and over, in circles, and in that spiral dance, the child inside me kicks, then quiets down, as if she is a rider of a horse, flanking the horse ahead. The girl keeps tugging at me, to the east, to the east. The contractions start. To the east, not here, to the east, the girl sings. My child is too early, two moon cycles before a child is supposed to come out. I try to tell the child inside me, not yet, not yet, it is not time yet, we must stay together, not yet. But the child inside me stubbornly moves around, the contractions move in the rhythm of the heartbeat, trying to pry us apart. The girl stands near me, stands over me. She looks at me quietly, her eyes indifferent, her eyes distant as if she is talking to the child inside me, but I cannot hear what they are talking about.

To the east, the child-god told him. To the west, the child-god whispered. It did not make sense to the man; he only knew that he was slipping. A seagull flew over him, catching the wind, gliding, then shitting, white slime landing on the man, but he was too tired to wipe it off. Then he realized that there must be a land, a land somewhere close by, for seagulls did not stray too far away from the land. Are we in a new world, he asked the child-god, and the child-god clicked her tongue in delight, no, you're back where you started. The man tried to raise his body, but his arms did not listen; he tried to see, but he could not raise his neck. He had drunk his own urine, he had licked his own sweat, only to come back to the land he had left. His curiosity took him nowhere except home. This is what you wanted, dead man, now die, said the child-god, die so that I can follow your soul to see the worlds you go to. And his heart stopped; he felt himself dying.

The contractions have started; I squat down, holding on to the branch. The girl keeps telling me to be quiet, to hush so that they won't find us. Hush, you'll get us caught, and we are so close to the border, hush. We're right by the steel machines, they'll crush us if you cry. Please keep it quiet, she sings, but I cannot, no matter how much I try to hush. Screams escape from me, involuntarily, screams in the rhythm of contraction. Please, please don't make any sound, or I'll have to kill you, she threatens, that's what Mama told me, if I make any sound when the Enemy is around, she'll have to kill me. It's better than being found out and getting killed, she said, Mama said that she'll kill me like a pig. I look at the girl between contractions, I do not know who she is. She has taken on a faraway look, her eyes unfocused and far away. I did what Mama told me to do, not make any sound, but Mama was found because she made sound. They dragged her by her hair, then they put a gun inside of her, where you're hurting right now, and kept laughing, saying that there's one bullet there, it's a roulette, a game, and they kept pulling the trigger, once, then a second time, and Mama just kept screaming and jerking every time they pulled the trigger. Mama kept begging and begging but they just kept laughing at her and kept pulling the trigger, and finally, the gun fired for real, and her stomach exploded, but she kept screaming and screaming even after her stomach broke open. My child began to slide down, head first, between me into the arms of the future. Footsteps begin all around me, my child's shoulders are out, and with the next contraction, her stomach. Footsteps crunch the leaves. Go, I tell the girl, go. The girl looks between my legs questioningly. Go, I tell her as my child shudders on the earth, our cord still purple and pulsing, blood spurting, reddening the leaves, the earth. Go, I don't think I can go any further. Footsteps come closer and closer. Go, carry this story to the east, I tell her, go so that you can live because we cannot. The girl clicks her tongue, and disappears.

drowning land

As soon as dreams leave dreamers, abandoned or rejected like leaves in late autumn, brown and bogged with
rain, they find birds to fly with, and make their way over
the mountain; past the pasture where cows and time stand
so still a painter could've painted them as still life; past the
cows digesting their past slowly; and finally drop down to
land on the roof of a house where the boy sleeps. Then they
seep through the cracks, down the wide beam that holds
the house up, and drop into the boy's mouth that's slightly
open with a hint of snore. Dreams find their ways into the
boy's sleep. He dreams people's thrown-away dreams, nightmares where children hide under beds from imagined and
real monsters, daydreams of great riches and loves that get
interrupted by teachers who want facts, facts that they can
see, facts, nothing but facts. Moments so real, more real than

anything they know so that wherever they may be, whatever they may be doing, those things cease to matter. Call him a dream collector. He dreams them all. He sees all that is hidden underneath, hidden under the faces people put on in the mornings, as soon as they wake up, dreams that are too near to the heart that only at night do they dare to come out.

The boy does nothing but lie in his bed and sleep. In his sleep, he has lived many lives. He sleeps all day long, eats whenever he wakes up, but it is never too long. He goes back to his bedding as soon as he is done eating, curling up like a question mark. His mother says that he is a no-good son, a lazy boy, why can't you help around the house? Don't you want to be a good son to your old parents? Why don't you use the good health the gods have given you to help with the farming? She says this every day, from the time she is up to the time she goes to bed. The boy has learned to nod off as soon as he sees her, first stretching out like a cat whenever she raises her voice, or tweaks his ear, or on occasion, sweeps him like dust with her broom. He pretends that he cannot understand a word she's saying. And without understanding, anything can sound like a mermaid song. He pretends to be a bear during its winter sleep, its heartbeat slowed down so slow that it beats only twice a minute. Or perhaps a rock in the quiet brook. Just letting the water pass over the top of the boy. He just sleeps, and dreams of all the things people never remember.

A dream: He is now a young man. The heart shatters, breaking like branches under the weight of snow. Snaps. All the pain has piled up and up, until the branches bow and the tips touch the ground. And the heart breaks. Standing in the black field where fire has left nothing green, the young man cries until his body shakes. Until it stills. The young man does not speak. Only looks. Wind touches the trees as if to comfort them, but they do not rustle; they creak. Dried and charred from the fire. All gone. The fire has eaten everything in sight, leaving only the remains of what it has embraced, black and hard, brittle to the touch. The harvest. The cattle. Nothing left. Not one thing left to remind the young man of all the labor he has put in. Even his tears, which should have come out, have been sucked dry by the fire, fire that dries all moist things instantly. He stands still, wanting to understand the message of the gods, but the ground is silent. There are no birds in the sky, as if they, too, know that the ground is silent. He doesn't know how long he has been standing like that. Clouds part, and suddenly, the sun shines on the field. Underneath his feet, a worm wriggles out of dark earth. He picks it up gently with his fingers. It wriggles, trying blindly to free itself. And the young man laughs. Laughs until tears roll down his cheeks. Laughs so hard that he is crying. But no longer from pain. In hope.

A dream: Her legs no longer listen to her. The woman has become too old—most people lose their friends one by one because of death, but the woman has lost control of her own limbs one by one. Her legs no longer have the strength to carry her around, though she is as skinny as the little girl she once was. Day after day, she sits on her couch by the window and looks down onto the street three stories down. Day after day, she sees many people rushing by, hurrying to get to places only they know how to get to. She looks out. Her only friend, her husband, so old that wrinkles and sunspots cover his face like a mask, would sit with her for a few hours, too, holding her hand. They would sit and watch days pass before their eyes. Seasons turning, leaving the window and the room untouched. Day after day, there would be a little girl in braids passing the window at the same time. She is first a little girl in braids wearing a pair of stockings, then she becomes a young girl in a ponytail and rolled-down socks, then a young woman with short hair and transparent panty-hose. The old man and woman watch her grow up with the years, loving her as a grandchild they never had. They never talk about her, just watch her, each with separate love, each with a separate understanding of her. And the young woman never knew about the two pairs of eyes that watched her grow up. One day, right in front of the window, the handle of her big bag breaks, spilling her notebooks and makeup on the street. Both the old woman and man gasp, wanting to help her gather her stuff before hurrying feet trample everything. The young woman quickly scoops down, rescuing her little possessions from the trampling. Suddenly, she stops. She feels someone close to her, and the little voice in her head says, Look up, look up or you will miss this. She looks up. For the first time, she looks up and sees an old woman and man looking down from the third floor of the rundown building she always walks by. Then the world slows down suddenly, the old woman and man unfocused, blurry; instead, the moment focuses on a young man with a bowler hat, looming over the young girl, blocking the window, curtaining the old couple completely now, and he asks the young girl, can I help you? She blushes. The old woman and man hold each other's hands tighter. Soon, the old woman dies, followed by the old man.

A dream: The only thing he can see is the sky. Lying on his back, the sky moves, clouds passing over him as if the world could care less about a man dying. It doesn't care. If he could touch the sky, he would. If he could touch his wife once again, he would. But even if he could, he wouldn't trade the view with anything else. He feels small, but also, he understands that he is dying because he must, as anything else, as clouds that must move on.

So he sleeps on and off for three years, gathering dreams like an avid collector, pigeonholing them in his memory.

Loss goes here, love goes here, hope goes here, loneliness goes here. In the end, each dream can go into each hole. They are all the same, all the things humans experience in one lifetime. And they are all his, and yet they are everyone's, if anyone chooses to want to look at them, or to understand them. Everyone is too busy to look, working hard just to live for one day. If they cannot keep their own dreams, how can they—why would they want to look at someone else's dreams? Only someone like the boy, who has no real life of his own, can toy around with it. His mother, when he tries to share these dreams he has seen, says that he is a dreamer and that he doesn't know anything. He is just a dreamer, impractical and useless. To him, all the dreams he sees are as real, more real than his house, his mother. All these told more about people than they ever dared to say. All the pain he felt in different dreams is real and his heart has broken so many times. And the laughter filled him up.

One day, he dreams no dream. He hears a voice by his ear, a whisper, really, that someone might have mistaken it for wind passing through the whirligig. It's time to wake up. He gets up from his bedding. Through the doorway and into the front yard, he stumbles. The sun blinds his eyes, and he staggers under the weight of such brightness. From one darkness, his eyes slowly readjust to the bright light he is not used to. Slowly, he sees dark shapes of people working in the faraway fields, most bent in the middle, shouldering the whole sky as they reach down to the ground and tenderly touch the green buds wilting under the heat. Everything bows under the brutal sun. He shades his eyes and begins to walk toward them, and as marionettes pulled by invisible strings, village children follow behind him, some laughing, some yelling out, the lazy boy has woken up after three years of sleep, the lazy no-good boy has woken up. He does not hear anything. Soon, rocks follow him from behind, slivering the air and pelting his back. He does not feel them thudding on his back. He just walks on until he reaches the edge of the village where the stream lies. The stream is too low for the season. Crops have wilted. The winter will be harsh.

He kneels on the ground and puts his ear against the ground. Children stop throwing rocks at him. He moves a foot away, kneels again. All the adults have unbent themselves, looking at him from their fields. The boy presses his ear again. Everything is quiet. Even birds have stopped in mid-flight. Only a swallow in the sky. The boy presses his ear. He hears something faint, something rushing under him. He lays his palm down and feels the ground. The same voice he heard earlier says, Here. The boy gets up as suddenly as he has gotten up suddenly from his three year long sleep, and runs home. Runs into the shed and grabs a hoe and runs back to where the sound is, little off the stream. With a hoe, he breaks the dry earth. He keeps digging and digging. The adults start to laugh, some making twirling signs by their heads. The boy's mother, when she realizes that her son is the center of the attention, runs to him and grabs his arms as he is about the strike the stubborn ground again. Stop it, what are you doing? He pushes her aside and keeps digging. Everyone stands still. He keeps digging and digging as the summer sun eats his white neck, turning it bright red with a sheet of sweat over it.

One by one, children begin to run home to get shovels, hoes, axes, anything that will break open the earth. Soon, adults begin to wander away from where they are toward the edge around the cluster of children hacking the ground. They, too, after watching, begin to dig the earth. The hole has become a crater, deeper than three adult men put together, wider than the path leading to the edge of the village. And they keep digging. No one says a word. The whole village raises their arms in the same rhythm, in the rhythm of two beats, up, down, up, down. Drop them strongly on the downbeat. As the boy strikes the earth one more time, the water begins to seep through, spreading out like a river, spreading out like the sky the boy had once seen in his dream.

There is water for the field; winter will be kind.

notes

"Grafting" is based on a Japanese folktale, "Ubasute-ya-
ma" (literal translation: "The Mountain Where You Abandon Your Old Mother"), which appears in various versions in
many regions. With its Chinese and Hindu roots, the origin
of the story is obscured in history and by time, but the main
storyline remains faithful in its various incarnations: the
old people must be left to fend for themselves in the natural
world.

"Autobiography" is based on the plight of countless Manchurian colonists at the end of World War II, when the So-
viet Union broke its treaty with Japan and attacked the border of Manchuria. The colonists, without the Japanese army
to defend them, were left on their own to make their escape
southward. Many perished by their own hands during the escape—usually parents killing their children rather than having to live the life of shame, and more died during the year
when they waited in camps to be repatriated. Some "sold"
their children so that their children could live instead of dying from dysentery, malnutrition, and starvation. Widowed
and young women often sold themselves into marriage to
Chinese men in order to survive in a land where they did not
speak the language, or for their families to survive with a fistful of money received as dowry. Even sixty-five years after the
war (2010), the former children of Japanese colonists, who
were sold or abandoned in China during the postwar chaos,
come to Japan to look for their parents and relatives. There
are said to be about 110,000 of them still living in China.

"Confession" is based on the B and C war criminal trials of the former Japanese soldiers and civilians, which took place in areas formerly occupied by the Imperial Japanese Army and Navy. Over a thousand men were executed. These trials are sometimes criticized as the "victors' trial." Many cases of executions of Allied aviators by civilians occurred in Germany and Japan, most of which were tried after the war.

"How We Touch the Ground, How We Touch" is based on the Japanese crypto-Christians who went underground after Christianity was banned in Japan in the early 17th century. The believers often presented themselves as Buddhists in public, and kept their faith secret codifying the Latin liturgy and prayers into the already existing Buddhist chants, changing names of the Holy Trinity and embedding the Christian icons into the Japanese architecture and sculptures. These crypto-Christians were often tested of their faith by being forced to step onto the icons of Jesus and the Virgin Mary and often, they did, in order to save themselves.

"Drowning Land" is loosely based on a Japanese fairy tale, "Sannen Netarou" (literal translation: "Taro Who Slept for Three Years") about a boy who slept for three years on and off, and using his wits, goes from rags to riches.

B orn in Tokyo and raised in Europe and America, Mariko
Nagai studied English at New York University. Her nu-
merous honors include the Erich Maria Remarque Fellowship
from New York University, fellowships from the Rockefeller
Foundation Bellagio Center, UNESCO-Aschberg Bursaries
for the Arts, Yaddo, and Djerassi. She has received Pushcart
Prizes both in poetry and fiction. Nagai's collection of po-
ems, *Histories of Bodies*, won the Benjamin Saltman Prize
from Red Hen Press. She teaches creative writing and literature at Temple University, Japan Campus in Tokyo.

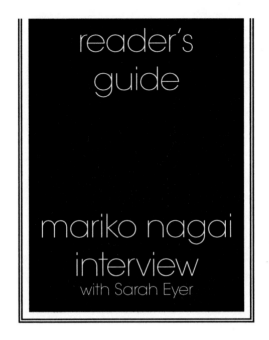

reader's
guide

mariko nagai
interview
with Sarah Eyer

*What drew you to reinventing the georgic—a pastoral form
of poetry—for this collection? Do you view these stories as a
different kind of poetry?*

The land is unforgiving. This is what I learned
growing up on a farm, though given that it is in the
middle of Tokyo, to call it a farm may be misleading.
The morning started out not with the sun—for the
sun was blocked by apartment buildings surround-
ing the farm—but with the hens clucking in fear
as my grandmother walked amidst them, kicking
them as she walked by. Her stubbornness rooted
her to the way of life on the land, though all around
her people were giving up the family land that
they'd had for so many generations in exchange for
large amounts of cash; the kind of money that they

would not have seen if they'd relied only on farming. Her view of the land was molded by the land, by the farm: the usefulness of a person lasted as long as his/her productivity did. She was a hard, practical woman who did not tolerate the body's weaknesses, who could not understand beauty because, to her, beauty represented the impractical; and the only thing that she understood was the practicalities of everyday life, where the land was demanding, where her livelihood depended on how much she gave. This is where stories in *Georgic* originated—the village of my imagination; not the idyllic notion of the harmonious, the *pastoral*, but in a Virgilian sense, where tension between men and the land was as real as probable famine, where men's faces were ravished by the elements, their backs molded by the earth, and their lives bound to the fate of the land. This is the world that emerged out of the confinement of the defined boundary, where demarcation of the village was clearly defined by a rock, by a tree, a signifier, and once anyone stepped outside it, he/she was forever marked as belonging to the otherworld, and could never be a part of the village even when he/she returned. And to stay a part of the collective, all of an individual's thoughts and secrets had to be guarded as closely to the heart as possible in order to survive in this environment. In many ways, this is a homage to Virgil who, so many centuries ago, captured the voice of farm life with all of its joys and heartbreaks.

These stories are filled with emotional land mines—almost impossible decisions coupled with extreme adversity. Was it difficult to write through those situations, and how do you put yourself in the mindset to write them?

I would be lying if I said that it is easy for me to slip into these characters' mindsets; even now, I'm not sure how successful I am in capturing the thought process that leads them to make certain choices that they make within these stories. Working with historical facts and folktales is fascinating that way: *that* choice that they made is there for us to judge, to recoil, and in some cases, dismiss by saying that *you* would never make that choice. Instead, I look at the result, and go backward into their lives and imagine what led them to make those choices: social context, historical mores, and, sometimes, current affairs, triggering insights into the inner lives of these characters. And what I found, through these stories, is that it is easy to judge the choices, but that these are choices that we ourselves would make, that *I* would make, if I were living in that time and given the understanding that I have of the world. *I* would be taking my aging mother to the mountain if my village commanded—where would I go, who would I be, if I were to defy the village, which is the only home I know, which is the only place in which I can exist—as is the case in "Grafting"? *I* would be selling my daughter to a stranger if I knew that she would have a chance to live—as is the case in "Autobiography." I would be killing an enemy aviator in vengeance if my daughter had been killed in an air raid during the war—as was the case in "Confession". No matter how much we can boast, saying that we are no longer medieval in our thinking and actions, that we have evolved so that we are civilized, we are lying to ourselves if we actually believe it—we really have not. We will also be making choices that are beyond words that we dare not utter, that we cannot ever tell anyone, when we are put in an impossible situation.

These stories are written from a variety of different perspectives, mostly women, but all come from different backgrounds, lifestyles, and regions; how did you create all these different voices?

Every "theme" demands a different form—and in the case of stories (if I know these are stories), then a voice would appear on its own. A typical story starts out with an image triggered by something that I read, or something that I saw. For example, in "Bitter Fruit," several pieces of information were floating around in my head without moorings: a 130-year-old photo of a Japanese prostitute sitting behind a trellised window, her face blurred but her anger in focus; a history of abortion and contraception in Japan; my obsession with public bath houses; a small rouge plant farm that I visited. And one day, several years ago, I was walking in Amsterdam early in the morning, which I like to do to see the real face of the city, and I came across this woman, a prostitute—not particularly striking—standing by her window, doing her business. What was striking about her was that it was early in the morning and she was working—just like drivers of these bread and produce trucks, people hurrying to work—and that, by the folds and wrinkles on her stomach, she had all the markings of having given birth. And on the floor, a baby was crawling. It was only a moment, but an image came together: a prostitute and a child sitting behind a trellised window, and the story was born.

The first story in this collection is "Grafting"—first published in New Letters *in 2002—from this did the others follow? Did you always know that you wanted to write a collection of short stories or did it happen spontaneously?*

The first story was a blessing and a curse. "Grafting" was my very first attempt at writing a short story and, for some reason, Robert Stewart, the current Editor in-Chief at *New Letters*, took it and published it and, to my surprise, it later won a Pushcart Prize. Unfortunately, it was beginner's luck—for a very long time, I kept writing stories that no one wanted to publish. It took a total of ten years from the initial conception of the first story to the actual publication of the book; only in the past three or so years did people finally start showing interest. With each story, I only thought in terms of an individual story—an individual universe, if you will—and worked at the consistency of language and the world that it contained. Three years into writing these stories, I began to see the thread that connected them, and that's when I knew that they belonged to a collection.

The collection begins and ends with the fickleness of agricultural life, starting with the absolute worst—complete adversity in the face of almost starvation. But with the final story, "Drowning Land," there is hope that the next winter will be a kind one. Was this something that you wanted to capture with the end story —the cyclical nature of agriculture?

It's a cliché, but everything around us is cyclical: seasons, hours, human lives. In many ways, I think of these individual stories—as well as the overall architecture of the book—as a cycle. Oftentimes, when I am working on a project – be it a poem or a story – I think of the project in terms of a musical movement. In the story, "Fugue," I explore the tension between repetition and variation. In music, a fugue must always introduce a theme or a subject, and voices enter, imitating the subject. But no voice is the same, no matter how much we try to approximate to the original theme. An inevitable variation occurs. For me, the idea of fugue, whether I've successfully conveyed it or not, is similar to human lives: we are only allowed one theme: we are born, we live, and we die; thus, the repetition of a theme. But the part that interests me the most, the part that makes life and literature interesting and amazing, is the part of "living"—so many infinite possibilities and improbabilities, so many variations that can be rendered from a theme. Our lives are a repetition of the lives before, but, at the same time, singular in their variations by the choices that we make. These choices are infinite, influenced by who we are, what we are, where we are. That's what makes us human, and vulnerable, and perhaps, forgivable at the end.

Many of these stories are based on events in Japanese history, such as the treatment of war criminals, and events at the end of World War II. Some stories are also based on Japanese folklore. What was your artistic inspiration behind framing these tragic historical events? How did you go about incorporating your research into your fiction?

I was a history minor as an undergraduate, so the idea of history, memory, and how we remember are big questions that I have. Though we may not be conscious of the linear time movement of history, we are in history as well as of history—but history, in a sense, refers to linear time movement, not necessarily defined in a conventional way. What I mean by that is that in our everyday lives, we go about our days, not really conscious of history until a catastrophic event occurs and, for those who experience such an event, it could almost become the *defining moment*. For victims of the Hiroshima and Nagasaki atomic bombs, their lives are divided into two time periods: before and after the bomb; for the mother in "Confession," her defining moment was not when she killed the enemy aviator, but the day that her daughter was killed in the air raid. That's why she does not remember whether or not she did actually kill the American pilot; for her, the defining moment has already occurred, and whatever happened afterward—and one can even say, the rest of her life—is colored by that event. But, of course, there are other influences in constructing the story: reading a book of interviews of former Japanese Imperial soldiers who participated in the rape and needless butchering of civilians during World War II back to back with a book of interviews of victims of the same event. How they remember, how they construct their narrative, and the positioning of "I" are heartbreaking: first of all, there are so many eyewitness accounts of rapes during wartime—both by the victims and from the third-party perspective. Account after account. The focus of their life narrative is about the rape—before and after. But there is so little from the rapists themselves—or if there is, it's usually mentioned in an offhand way; but the emphasis, the narrative, is almost always about how they themselves suffered as soldiers. An earlier version of "Confession"—a version that remained for five years or so—was a narrative from a Salem witch. It was a failure of a story, but I just could not admit that to myself. But as soon as I made that connection—of the perpetrator and the victim and how they view an event—an image of a woman looking for her daughter amidst the rubbles arose, and that moment, for her, was the defining moment.

I'm a voracious consumer of information, and the more down-to-earth it is, the more excited I get. It's not the political decisions, which general did what, or the historical figures that concern me, but rather the everyday people and how they lived, what worldviews they held, what choices they were forced to make. Used bookstores and antique shops; archives and little museums; cemeteries and churches; out-of-print books and letters sold on eBay. I keep all these in my head, some consciously and most unconsciously, and one day, something happens and an image emerges like a dream or a life that I could have led. All I need to do is to listen carefully, attentively, to what is not apparent, to put aside all the judgments that I harbor consciously and unconsciously, and to let these characters whisper their stories to me. That's when history becomes a story, and out of the story, rises compassion.

questions for discussion

1. Many of the stories in *Georgic* draw their inspiration from historical events, such as the plight of Manchurian colonists following World War II, trials of war criminals, and the suffering of Japanese crypto-Christians. Does your awareness of this historical basis for some of the stories affect how you respond to them as fiction? What larger questions do the stories raise about humanity in general?

2. These stories use many different strategies, including multiple viewpoints and short vignettes. One example is "Love Story," which contains several vignettes. How does love tie each of these vignettes together into one story? How does Nagai interweave love and tragedy?

3. The georgic is a type of poetry, for which Virgil was known, dealing with the practical aspects of rural life. Why do you think Nagai chose this title for one of the stories and for the book as a whole?

4. How does the clear, unsentimental tone of Nagai's writing affect the way you feel the impact of its events?

5. Though *Georgic* is a story collection rather than a novel, what do you see as the central thread that unites these stories?

6. Most of the narrators in *Georgic* are unnamed women— one is called Monkey (in "Bitter Fruit"). What are some of the challenges that these characters face as women?

7. One character must sell her daughter in the hopes her daughter's life will be better; another must leave her aging mother in the woods because there is not enough food for the village. What do you see as the most difficult or haunting choice characters must face in this book?